Lost in the freezing cold woods— can things possibly get worse?

At the top of the hill, Katie looked down and saw a wide creek at the bottom. Its rushing water burbled noisily over and around the rocks and boulders in its path. Pink and yellow lights from the setting sun glinted here and there like faint jewels.

Beautiful as it was, Katie shook her head forlornly. They had definitely not passed this creek on the way in. She was way off course.

Yet . . . maybe the creek would lead her somewhere. Following it was worth a try, anyway.

Katie started down the hill toward the creek. After that, everything happened in a fast jumble. Her foot slid on a muddy spot and shot out from under her. She felt herself tumble forward and bang her head on a rock.

She grabbed wildly for something to hold onto, but there was nothing. She was sliding, sliding, sliding down the steep hill toward the rushing water below.

Katie's Angel

FOREVER ANGELS

Katie's Angel

Suzanne Weyn

Troll

For Diana Gonzalez with love

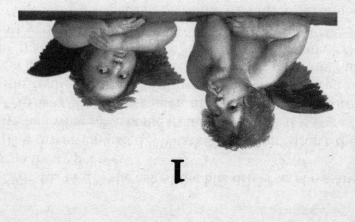

1

"Yeah, well, same to you, frog-breath!" Katie snarled over her shoulder at Darrin Tyson, the boy who sat in the seat behind her on the bus.

"Who you calling names?" he challenged, swaggering to his feet. With his barrel chest and spiky, short blond hair, he looked like some kind of mutant terminator.

"You, mush-for-brains," said Katie, levelly, not even bothering to turn around this time. "I'm not changing seats with anybody. You're not king of the bus."

"New kids don't get to sit in the back until I give permission," Darrin insisted.

"Oh, dry up," Katie told him with a contemptuous glare. "I'll sit wherever I want."

With a grinding of gears, the beat-up yellow school bus finally rattled to a stop at the end of a long dirt drive. With a final, fierce glance at the boy, Katie strode up the aisle. She hesitated a moment once she reached the door. Chunks of ice the size of gravel bounced wildly around on the dirt path before her.

"What is *that?*" she asked the bus driver as she stared at the frosty pebbles.

The driver chuckled. "What's the matter? Don't they have hail where you come from?"

"No way. I've never seen anything like it before," Katie replied. In all the thirteen years she'd lived on West 68th Street, she had definitely never seen anything like this weird ice storm. "Welcome to the country," she muttered under her breath.

"Well, are you getting off?" the bus driver prodded. "You can't stand there forever. I have to get moving."

Katie wriggled out of her khaki backpack and held it over her head.

Darting out into the hailstorm, Katie ran hard, her long legs pumping. Her straight hair flew behind her like a soft, brown cape. "Ow!" she yelled as a hailstone stung her ankle. The backpack slipped, and another grazed her cheekbone.

I'm going to get creamed out here, she decided, ducking for cover under one of the full, thick-trunked pine trees on the right of the drive. She leaned back against the nubbly bark and tried to catch her breath.

It had been a tough day. Now the weather seemed like the last straw. Katie bit her lip and blinked quickly. She didn't cry. She never cried. Not anymore. Roughly, she brushed at her eyes.

"Hail," she muttered. *This place would have chunks of ice that attacked you from the sky,* she thought. Every dumb, annoying thing in the world was here in Pine Ridge. Why should hail surprise her?

Katie threw her pack on the ground and knelt to

unzip it. She pulled a battered baseball cap out and tugged it onto her head. Then she rummaged until she found a pack of Camel cigarettes and a plastic yellow Bic lighter.

So far she hadn't smoked any of the cigarettes. She'd bought the pack at Penn Station while she'd waited for the train to bring her here to Pine Ridge. All the tough kids she saw in the city smoked. Just having the pack made her feel tough. And that's what she wanted to be—needed to be—right now. Tough.

Besides, just letting the pack be seen around school let kids know she was the kind of person they shouldn't mess with.

Most of them seemed to have gotten the message. They left her alone. They weren't friendly, but they didn't bug her, either. That was the important thing. She could live without friends, but she had to make sure they didn't try to push her around just because she was new. All the kids left her alone, except for Darrin.

"What a jerk," Katie muttered, thinking of Darrin. Just because he was bigger than the other eighth-graders, he thought he owned the world. Well, he wasn't going to push her around.

Katie gazed down at the small, brown camel on the cigarette pack. It looked exotic and faraway.

Katie imagined herself in a hot, windy desert. Sand crunched underfoot as she swayed atop her camel. She was warm; she was dry; she was surrounded by fragrant breezes and the cheerful sound of a bustling open-air marketplace as colorfully garbed vendors sold shining brasses, boldly flowing silks, pungent spices.

It was a far cry from the grim reality. Katie hunched further into her thin jacket. An ironic smile drew up the right corner of her wide, full lips. This was probably as good a time as any to start smoking.

Why not?

Who cared? No one. It was true. There wasn't anybody left who cared what she did. So why not?

Tossing back her hair, Katie flipped her thumb along the wheel of the lighter. She stuck a cigarette in her mouth and cupped her hands around the lighter's flame to try to light it. She was just about to try actually inhaling to light it when, suddenly, she froze.

She'd heard something. Was it a branch snapping in the wind?

Or a footstep?

There it was again!

Slipping the lighter in one pocket, the cigarette in another, she turned to face the woods behind her. The slow crunching sound came again.

Katie balanced on the balls of her feet, her senses fully alert. Her lively amber brown eyes scanned the woods. Who was sneaking up on her?

All around, the hailstones continued to beat the ground, making a steady clacking sound. The pine branches gently rustled together in the wind.

Katie's gaze finally fell on a spot to her right, about three yards away. It was a circle about four feet across in which everything was completely still.

The branches above the circle were unruffled by the wind.

No hail fell inside the circle.

The only movement—if you could call it that—was dancing spots of sunlight coming from some break in the overcast sky. The unlikely light, like weird sunny bubbles, made its way down through the dense tree branches to the otherwise shady forest floor below.

Katie stared in bewilderment at the windless spot of sparkling light. Quietly, slowly, she moved toward the golden circle.

She stood a moment outside the quivering light and looked up. How had light found its way down through the thick blanket of clouds above? This was truly strange, even otherworldly. *Maybe she should just leave*, she thought. Yet something inside her felt pulled toward that incredible circle of light and calm.

As Katie stepped into the spot, a strange sensation overcame her. *What's happening to me?* she wondered. Her breathing became deeper and longer. Her tense shoulders relaxed.

And she sensed—strongly sensed—that she wasn't alone.

This feeling surprised her. She wasn't someone who imagined things. She usually laughed at people who thought they saw ghosts or claimed to hear eerie noises in the dark.

But this feeling was so strange.

And so real.

"Mom?" Katie asked with a catch in her voice. "Mom, are you here?"

She wasn't sure why she'd said that. The words just tumbled from her lips.

It was an intuition, a hunch.

Katie turned in a slow circle, vaguely aware that she could no longer feel the cold wind blowing down the neck of her jacket. "Mom? . . . Dad, is it you?"

It *had* to be one of them.

A fierce happiness flooded her. Somehow she'd known they'd find her again, no matter what it took. She never really believed they would just disappear from her life the way they'd seemed to.

Barely daring to breathe, she listened and looked, waiting for some sign.

But if they were there, why didn't they let her know, say something, show themselves?

"Please," she pleaded, her voice almost a sob.

But no sign came.

Tears welled in Katie's eyes. She ached with the need to blink them out, but still she wouldn't give in. Katie did not cry.

Of course there was no sign, she thought, despairing. Her parents weren't there. They weren't there, and they were never coming back.

What an idiot she was to have imagined they were actually present!

Katie ran out of the circle and back onto the drive. Hailstones struck her mercilessly as she tore up toward the house. Hard bits of frost and hail crackled under her hiking boots.

She didn't care anymore about the stinging hailstones. She just needed to run, to put distance between herself and that bit of windless light she'd made such a fool of herself over.

After about three minutes, she slowed down, panting.

The windy sky seemed to slow down along with her, shooting out only the occasional hailstone.

Catching her breath, Katie looked at the tall, tumble-down, dirty white house at the end of the muddy dirt drive. *What a mess*, she thought as she gazed at the house, with its sagging roof and broken shingles.

A last hailstone hit Katie on the head. Cold as she was, somehow she just couldn't bear to go inside the house just yet.

She knew what she'd find, and she couldn't deal with it. Not yet.

2

Katie couldn't face seeing Aunt Rainie and Cousin Mel just yet. She wasn't in the mood for it. She was *never* in the mood for it. They were so different from any people she'd ever met. She couldn't get used to them at all.

Besides, she couldn't stop thinking about that spot in the woods. The memory of that weird calm was still with her somehow. She needed to be alone a little while longer. She wanted to hold onto the feeling before all the noise, smells, and bustle of life inside her aunt's house wiped it all away.

She walked past the house to a dilapidated rusty-colored building several yards away. Pushing in the peeling red door, she stepped inside. Dim gray light filtered down from the grimy, broken window high over her head. Ranged along the unpainted plank walls were haphazard piles of disassembled old farm machinery and rusted car parts. Dusty piles of magazines sat collecting more dirt and grit. A broken dining room table leaned to one side, and its two remaining right legs jutting out reminded Katie of a wounded animal fallen to its knees. The cracked cement floor crunched underfoot with its covering of dirt and old leaves.

A faded, frayed, rose-patterned chair sat in the corner. Its back was humped and lumpy with age, and frazzled rose-pink fringe edged the bottom. When Katie looked at it she could see the lovely, soft chair it had once been. Nicked dark wood framed the back and the torn arms. *Who had let it get into such a mess? Couldn't her aunt and uncle see how beautiful this chair was?* Katie wondered again, as she wondered every time she looked at the chair. Her mother would have had that chair recovered and polished in an instant. Her mother had been smart about things like that.

Not Aunt Rainie. Aunt Rainie wouldn't be able to see the beauty hidden in this chair even if it somehow managed to walk up and stomp on her fat feet.

In the six weeks since she'd come to live with Aunt Rainie and Uncle Jeff, Katie had spent a lot of time in this chair. She called it her thinking chair. It was a comfortable place to sit and be alone when she needed to sort things out.

She understood the chair. It had once had a beautiful life with people who appreciated and loved it. And now its life was ruined. It was stuck out here, rundown and unloved, in a crummy barn belonging to people who had no idea of its value.

It was just like Katie.

She plunked down in the chair, dropping her pack to the floor. Closing her eyes, she let her head fall back against the top of the chair and envisioned what it would have been like if her parents had really appeared to her back there among the pine trees.

It was easy to imagine. She saw her tall, slim mother with her shining brown hair and casually stylish clothing.

How she missed her mother's gentle eyes and ready smile.

She could see her father, too, tall and broad-shouldered, with the same amber brown eyes as her own.

She pictured them putting their arms around her and leading her back home to their apartment house on West 68th Street.

Her friend Addy would come by, and they'd play video games until her mother offered to take them for pizza at the corner. After they walked Addy home, she and her mother would go back to their apartment and work on the huge jigsaw puzzle they kept set up in the living room while they watched a movie on TV.

That's what her life had been like before—so safe, so normal. Some people thought life in the city was dangerous. But it had never felt that way to Katie. The city was where her family and friends were. The city was the only place she'd ever known, until now.

She knew she should be more grateful to Aunt Rainie and Uncle Jeff for taking her in after the car crash. She'd probably be in a foster home now if they hadn't. She shuddered to think how much worse *that* would have been.

Aunt Rainie was her mother's half sister. She and

Katie's mother had had different mothers. Aunt Rainie was much older than Katie's mother. They'd never lived together, and they weren't close. "We took you because family is family," Aunt Rainie explained to her. "You can't let family go to strangers."

Sometimes Katie couldn't help wondering if "going to strangers" really would have been worse. After all, who could be stranger than Aunt Rainie, Uncle Jeff, and Cousin Melvin?

A noise coming from the corner of the barn startled Katie away from her bleak thoughts. Leaning forward in the chair, she looked toward the corner of the barn. The sound came again, and she realized it was coming from behind a pile of dried, splintered wood.

Her heart pounded as she got up from her chair. Was it a rat? She'd seen one scurry around the back of this building the first week she was here.

Her senses alert once again, she crept lightly to the corner.

She heard the sound again from behind the wood. Leaning across the woodpile to look, she let out her breath and laughed shakily.

Myrtle, Aunt Rainie's fat gray cat, sat looking up at Katie from an old dresser drawer that had somehow become parted from its dresser. Myrtle was surrounded by five mewing balls of gray, black, and white fluff.

"How cute," Katie murmured, reaching down and lifting up one of the kittens. She held the soft, warm furball to her cheek. It purred as if it had a tiny engine inside it.

Myrtle meowed complainingly up at Katie. "Do you

want your baby back?" Katie asked playfully as she lowered the kitten back into the drawer. As she straightened back up over the woodpile, several pieces of wood tumbled from the top of the pile.

Katie jumped out of the way, then knelt to gather the planks. One of the pieces was wider than the others—about two feet wide. It had writing carved into it. Angels Crossing, it said.

Katie thought of all the Deer Crossing signs she'd seen since coming here to Pine Ridge. The sign brought to her mind an image of gorgeous winged angels crossing a two-lane highway in single file, while cars idled impatiently, waiting for the unhurried angels to pass.

The idea of it made Katie smile as she ran her fingers along the carved letters.

Suddenly, with a rough squeal, the barn door opened. A tall man's shadow fell across the barn's gray light.

Katie looked up sharply and dropped the Angels Crossing sign.

3

"What's that?" demanded Uncle Jeff, stepping into the barn.

"I, uh, I, uh, just found this sign here," Katie replied, looking at the Angels Crossing sign at her feet. She wasn't sure why Uncle Jeff made her so nervous. Maybe it was the hard look in his steely gray eyes, or the way his deeply lined, leathery old face never melted into a smile.

He'd never been really mean to her, but Katie just knew he didn't want her there. After all, he wasn't exactly subtle about it. For one thing, every time he complained to Aunt Rainie about their bills, he glanced at her.

Now Uncle Jeff crossed the barn and bent to pick up the sign. Katie studied his rough, calloused hands. Years of working on farm machinery had made his hands almost look like machine parts themselves.

"Angels Crossing, huh," he said, reading the sign. "My sister, Trudie, carted this hunk of junk home one day from the woods over at Pine Manor. It came from some bridge or something."

"Why was the bridge called Angels Crossing?" Katie dared to ask, shreds of her own "angels crossing" fantasy still dancing in her mind.

Uncle Jeff shrugged. "Buncha nonsense, you ask me." He snorted. "I seem to recollect some fool story about a doorway for angels. Or some such. Buncha nonsense, I say. I'm surprised this thing didn't get burned for firewood years ago. What are you doing in here, anyway?" He looked at her curiously.

"Myrtle had kittens," she said, pointing over to the pile of wood.

Uncle Jeff looked down over the woodpile at the kittens and frowned. "More for the pound to give away or gas."

"Gas!" Katie cried.

"When I was a kid, my father used to drown the litters down at the creek behind the house."

"That's horrible!"

"You eat chicken, don't you?" said Uncle Jeff casually, walking back toward the door.

"Yeah," Katie said, not getting the connection.

"What's the difference? You kill a chicken, or you kill a kitten. They're both animals."

"I suppose, but . . ." Somehow it just didn't seem the same. "Maybe I can get kids at school to take some."

Uncle Jeff pushed open the barn door, then turned back to Katie. "Aunt Rainie will be wanting help with supper."

"All right," Katie agreed, silently praying that tonight wouldn't be *another* canned corned beef hash night.

Katie couldn't believe how much canned food she'd eaten since coming there. Considering how many farms were in the area, it was especially strange.

Katie's mother had been a big fresh food believer. She'd claimed most prepared food was just salt and chemicals. Katie's parents had even traveled by subway to the Greenmarket in Union Square once a week to get the farm-fresh fruits and vegetables sold there. Eating fresh food had been really important to them.

Aunt Rainie, on the other hand, hated to cook. In her opinion, cooking food that was already more or less cooked was the easiest way to get a hated job over with.

With an inward grimace, Katie grabbed her backpack off the floor and followed Uncle Jeff out of the barn. Even before the door to the house opened, Katie knew what she'd hear. Sure enough, as she stepped through the doorway, a blast of country music hit her ears.

"I loved you, girl. Or didn't you know?" some heartbroken singer whined. "How could you just run off with the rodeo? That bronco buster stole your heart. And now my whole world's falling apart. I loved you. Or didn't you know?"

Katie winced at the syrupy lyrics. She didn't mind the kind of country music they played on the video channels sometimes. But Aunt Rainie constantly listened to a kind of country music Katie had never heard before. It all sounded old and twangy, like it was written and recorded a long time ago—and Katie hated it.

A frying pan full of canned corned beef sizzled greasily on the stove.

Aunt Rainie sat on one kitchen chair with her thick ankles propped up on another, the phone cradled between her pudgy shoulder and chin. Her tightly permed, bleached blonde hair framed her broad, smiling face. "I'll have to call you back, June," she said. "I'll see you down at the beauty shop Friday. Bye now."

Aunt Rainie pecked Uncle Jeff's cheek with a kiss as he headed for the sink to wash his hands. "Everything go all right at school today, Katie?" she asked pleasantly.

"Okay," Katie answered laconically as she pulled off her jacket and dropped her backpack down on the floor by the door.

"Did you get caught in that hailstorm?" Aunt Rainie asked with a chuckle.

Katie frowned. What was so amusing about getting clobbered with stinging chunks of ice? She felt like screaming but forced herself to speak calmly. "Yeah. Does that happen around here much?"

"This time of year, end of winter, it's not that unusual," Aunt Rainie replied. "It's always sort of surprising when it happens, though. Something special about it, huh? I kind of get excited when it hails."

You would, thought Katie.

"Set the table, would ya, hon?"

"Sure," Katie agreed. Aunt Rainie wasn't really *that* bad. With her fat body stuffed into awful-looking polyester outfits, she looked worse than she was.

Aunt Rainie wasn't mean or anything. Katie had a hard time putting her finger on it. She was just so completely different from Katie's mother. It was almost impossible to believe they were sisters, even half sisters. Katie's mother had been a college teacher. She was always reading and talking about interesting things. Aunt Rainie seemed to live to gossip with her friends while they all hung out at the beauty parlor, where Aunt Rainie did shampoos.

"Rainie, I thought you said you were going to get Katie set up with after-school chores," Uncle Jeff said suddenly. "It's no good for a young girl to just be hanging around with nothing to do. I found her out in the barn just poking around."

"Oh, I'm still thinking about it, Jeff," Aunt Rainie answered him. "You were out in that dirty old barn, Katie? What on earth were you doing there?"

"Looking at Myrtle's kittens."

"I figured that's why I hadn't seen her in a few days," said Aunt Rainie. "Lord knows how we're going to get rid of these ones."

"I can always drop 'em in the crick," said Uncle Jeff as he dried his hands on a kitchen towel.

Could he possibly be serious?

"I'll give them away at school," Katie said quickly. "I know lots of kids who want kittens."

If her aunt and uncle recognized this as the total lie it was, they gave no sign. Out of the corner of her eye, Katie thought she could see Aunt Rainie looking at her, but when she turned, Aunt Rainie was busy poking at the mess on the stove with a big fork.

Uncle Jeff harrumphed.

"What's that, hon?" Katie couldn't believe how Aunt Rainie always acted like all Uncle Jeff's weird noises were actually some attempt at conversation. Funny thing was, he usually did answer her.

Now Katie was shocked to hear him say, "I said, save me a trip to the crick if Katie knows folks who want kittens."

Katie set the blue plastic plates down on the worn, white vinyl cloth on the kitchen table. She put out the plastic cups and the dull, mismatched flatware. She felt unreasonably happy for the first time in weeks, but she didn't dare let anyone see it.

Cousin Mel sauntered in from the living room, dressed in his usual grease-stained jeans and a dirty white undershirt. Leaning against the kitchen doorway, he scratched his protruding stomach and belched.

"Melvin!" Aunt Rainie scolded her twenty-year-old son, who towered over her.

Cousin Mel just pushed a clump of his dark hair out of his blue eyes and grinned down at her, pleased with himself.

Katie put paper napkins on the table without even saying hello to Mel. She'd given up trying to make conversation with him the first week she was there. He only answered her with grunts or one-word replies. He made it clear that he was completely disinterested in her. The only things that interested Mel were his beat-up Harley Davidson motorcycle and the car and motorcycle races on TV.

Aunt Rainie and Uncle Jeff had two grown daughters who were married and lived in the next town over, Miller's Creek. Katie had met them when she first arrived, but they hadn't been over since then.

Dizzy, Mel's dog, shuffled into the kitchen. Mel

quickly grabbed a clump of corned beef hash from the pan and threw it onto the scratched gray linoleum floor. In a flash Dizzy gobbled it.

Aunt Rainie just rolled her blue eyes helplessly.

Katie eyed the corned beef and her stomach lurched. Now that Mel had stuck his dirty fingers into it, it seemed twice as disgusting. Besides, by the time she got to eat it, it would be burned. It always was.

Katie suddenly felt that if she had to eat corned beef hash again tonight, she might be sick to her stomach.

"Aunt Rainie, I don't feel very good," she said. "Do you mind if I don't eat supper tonight?"

"Why sure, sweetheart," Aunt Rainie agreed. "You just go lie down."

Katie picked up her backpack from by the door and went upstairs to the room she'd been given at the end of the hall. Stepping inside, she tossed her pack onto her bed and sighed. *This had to be the ugliest room on earth*, she'd decided. The worst thing about the room was the wallpaper, a silver metallic paper with black-ink drawings of fat cupids flying around with their bows and arrows. The wallpaper curled up at the seams wherever two pieces met.

Katie threw herself onto her narrow twin bed and unzipped her pack. Pulling a piece of paper from her spiral notebook, she began a letter to her best friend, Addy.

Dear Addy,

I still consider you my best friend, but not for long if you don't write to me soon. I've been gone six weeks and written you three letters. All you've done is send me that dumb postcard from Disney World. Isn't thirteen a little old to still be hanging around with Goofy? Write me a real letter!!!! Okay???????? Did you lose my new address? I'll give it to you again at the end of this letter, just in case you did. I'm not writing any more until I get a real letter from you. So write!

Your friend,
Katie

Katie put down her pen but she still felt like writing. She wasn't going to write to Addy, though. They'd been really tight back in the city. Just because she wasn't there anymore, did that mean they were no longer friends? It was starting to look like Addy thought so.

Katie pulled a composition notebook out from beneath her mattress and boxspring. She opened it and began writing.

Dear Journal,
It's now six weeks since Mom and Dad took their long weekend to Montauk Point. The long, long weekend they never came back from—that they never will come back from.

She put down her pen and thought about the last time she'd seen her parents, the Friday afternoon when they'd dropped her off in front of Addy's apartment house. She'd hugged them both quickly as she stepped out of the car they'd rented for their trip. "See you Monday night," her father had said. "Be good."

Katie remembered she'd rolled her eyes at him.

Maybe she wouldn't have done that if she'd known it was the last time she'd ever see him.

In her head she understood what had happened. On Monday evening they'd been coming home in a bad rainstorm. A pickup truck going too fast in the oncoming lane had skidded out of control and crashed into them.

But in her heart Katie was still waiting for them to come back.

Katie clicked the top of her pen rapidly and then went back to writing.

Here are some questions I've been thinking about today. Are there such things as ghosts? I kind of thought there were, but I don't anymore. What about angels? Do you believe in them? I found this weird sign today about some kind of angels bridge. I guess somebody somewhere really thought angels were on that bridge. What idiots! When I was a little kid, I believed in angels. I even thought I saw my guardian angel once, but little kids are so dumb, with their imaginations and all.

Katie remembered the time she'd seen her guardian angel. She'd been five and proudly riding her new two-wheeler bike down a park path without realizing she had to push backwards on the pedals to stop. The bike rushed toward the street, gaining more and more speed every second.

Then, as if from nowhere, a woman stepped into her path. Katie remembered colliding into her and then crashing to the ground. Car brakes squealed in the background as she looked up into the woman's warm, smiling face with her large, startlingly blue eyes. The woman had long, straight black hair. And Katie remembered seeing wings. She remembered them clearly, vividly. Feathery, white wings, high and glistening, fanning out from behind her shoulders.

The next thing she knew, her mother was hugging her fiercely while some pale-faced, trembling stranger sobbed, "I thought I was going to hit her for sure."

"The angel lady stopped me," Katie had said. She'd expected the lady to be there. But the angel lady had disappeared.

Katie shook her head at the memory. "The angel lady stopped me," she repeated softly with a self-mocking smile. "What a dweeb I was back then. Little kids can be so weird." Obviously, some woman had come along, Katie had crashed into her, and the woman had kept going. But for some reason, Katie had thought she was an angel.

Katie laughed again at the memory. Kids thought up the goofiest stuff.

Her stomach growled, and she decided that eating the gross corned beef was better than starving. She closed her journal and slipped it back under her mattress.

As she went down the stairs, raised voices coming from the kitchen made her stop short.

"All I'm saying, Jeff, is that you could be a little warmer to her," Aunt Rainie said.

"She's not a particularly warm child," Uncle Jeff shot back, sounding annoyed.

"She's just lost her parents, for crying out loud," Aunt Rainie said, her voice rising higher. "That girl is still in a state of shock. I have not seen her cry even once. Not once! That just isn't normal."

"Normal is different for different people," Uncle Jeff said sulkily.

"Well, I don't think we need to be giving her chores right away," said Aunt Rainie. "Why are you so all fired anxious to put her to work?"

"The girl's one more mouth to feed around here, Rainie," Uncle Jeff exploded. "At least she can help earn her keep!"

"Be quiet, you old fool," Aunt Rainie hissed. "She'll hear you! And she'll think you mean it!"

Katie gripped the banister tightly. Their words seemed to float on the air and mingle with the greasy smell of the food. Together, they were too much for her. Suddenly, she really did feel sick to her stomach. Covering her mouth, she ran back upstairs to the bathroom.

"Katie, honey, is that you?" she heard her aunt's voice floating faintly up the stairs as she slammed the door.

4

"Oooohhhh, they are *too* adorable," cooed a dark-haired girl named Lizzie who sat in front of Katie in homeroom. She was looking at the Polaroid photo Katie had snapped that morning of Myrtle's newborn kittens. For the first time in weeks, Katie wasn't being totally ignored in school. She tried not to let herself give in to how good it felt.

"Want one?" Katie asked eagerly.

"Oh, no, I couldn't," Lizzie said mournfully. "My father is allergic."

Katie checked the door. Mr. Palmero, their homeroom teacher, hadn't come in yet. It would be great if she could get one of the kittens adopted before homeroom even began.

"What's that?" asked Darrin, the blond-haired bully from her bus. He turned in his seat in front of Lizzie and reached out for the photo.

"It's nothing," said Katie. She'd never give Darrin a kitten. He was the kind of guy who would probably do something terrible to it.

Darrin snatched the photo from Lizzie. "Ooooh, it's iddy-widdy-kitties," he said in a jeering voice. "I'll take them all. They're great fried."

Katie quirked the side of her lip at him disdainfully. "Very funny."

"No kidding, everyone around here eats kittens. Didn't you know that?" Darrin continued. "You know that Magic Meat they serve in the cafeteria. That's really kitten. Right, Lizzie?"

"You're gross," Lizzie replied.

"Give me the picture back," said Katie, holding out her hand.

"I don't want to give it back, new kid." Darrin always called her "new kid," and encouraged everyone else to do the same. Right from her first day at Pine Ridge Middle School, he seemed to take some strange delight in antagonizing her. "I told you, I want the kittens."

Lizzie took out her English literature book and began reading as Katie and Darrin talked across her desk.

"What would you do with kittens?" Katie asked contemptuously.

Darrin wiggled his eyebrows insanely. "You should try it, they're delicious," he said as he slipped the photo into his spiral notebook.

"Come on, dibwad, give it back," said Katie getting up from her seat.

"What did you call me?" Darrin taunted, smirking.

"You heard me," Katie said. "Now give me the picture."

A petite girl with wild, carrot-red curls that tumbled around her shoulders, and a face full of pale freckles, turned in her seat in front of Darrin. "Why don't you just stop being a jerk and give it to her, Darrin," said the girl. Her name was Ashley, Katie remembered.

"Oh, now I'm a jerk, too?" Darrin said. "Thank you. You girls are so sweet."

"Darrin! Oh, gross! What's that on your shoe?" Ashley cried, her green eyes wide with revulsion.

Darrin looked down sharply, and in that moment, Ashley grabbed for his spiral notebook. In a flash, Darrin saw that his shoe was fine and tugged the notebook back from her. The photo flew to the floor and Darrin snapped it up. He jumped up, standing in the aisle between his desk and the window. "What about it, new kid, do I get the kittens or not?"

"Yeah, sure, like she's really going to give you one, Darrin," said Ashley derisively. "Does she look totally out of her mind to you? Because no sane person would ever let you near anything that helpless."

Katie glanced at Ashley and was surprised to see her nod emphatically and smile. She had never spoken to Ashley much, but she seemed like one of the cooler kids in the class. Katie was grateful, now, for Ashley's help.

"Seriously, I don't really want them all, I just want one," Darrin wheedled, his blue eyes slit with nasty laughter. "I'm just dying for a kitty sandwich on a bun!" He pushed up one of the windows, letting in a current of cold air. "Promise me one or I throw your kitty photo out the window."

"Dork," Ashley muttered. "We're only on the first floor. Or didn't you notice that?"

"Who cares?" said Darrin. "It will blow away before

she can get outside to get it. So what about it, new kid? Do I get a kitten or what?"

For a moment, Katie was almost tempted to promise him a kitten. But she could never have done that to a poor, innocent creature. Besides, she really resented being intimidated like this.

"I'd rather die than give you a kitten," Katie told him defiantly.

Still smiling, Darrin held the photo out the first-floor window and let it flutter away.

Katie rushed to the window. "I don't believe you did that," she cried angrily.

"I told you I would," said Darrin, taking his seat. "There's nothing you can do about it now."

Katie felt like slapping the smug smile right off his ugly face. He was so pleased with his nasty little trick, so sure he'd gotten the best of her. She could always take another picture, of course, but it galled her to be picked on like this. She couldn't let him get away with it.

Looking out the window, she could just see the photo fluttering a few feet away, stuck in the dense leaves of a bayberry bush. It would be easy enough to just climb out the window and get it.

Checking the door, she saw no sign of Mr. Palmero yet. But the homeroom bell would ring any moment, which didn't give her much time. She pushed the window all the way up and threw one long leg over the ledge.

"Don't tell me you're going after it?" Darrin asked in disbelief.

"Hey, it's cold," complained a boy nearby.

Everyone in class was watching alertly to see what was happening.

"I'll watch for Mr. Palmero," offered Ashley.

Katie kicked her other leg over, turned, and dropped lightly to the ground. A shiver of cold wind ran through her as she quickly plucked the Polaroid from the bush and stuck it safely in the back pocket of her jeans.

In order to reach the window ledge from the ground, Katie had to balance on a small brick wall that ran around the base of the building. She stepped onto it, grabbed hold of the window ledge, and tried to pull herself back up. But something was wrong. She was stuck on something, one leg held in place down around her ankle.

"Hurry, Katie," Ashley said, sticking her head out the window.

"I can't. I'm stuck on something."

"Try going back down," Ashley suggested.

Slowly, Katie lowered herself back to the ground, but her one leg remained hooked at the top of the brick. Examining it, Katie saw that a bent construction staple sticking out between the brick edge and school's siding had somehow snagged the hem of her jeans.

She tried to work the fabric, but the sharp edge of the staple refused to come free.

Ashley dropped to the ground beside her just as the homeroom bell rang. "Hurry up," she said urgently, bending to where the fabric was caught. "Can't you get it unstuck?"

"I'm going to have to tear them," Katie said.

"Too bad. They're nice jeans, too," Ashley sympathized.

"Ripped jeans are in style," Katie said, yanking her leg firmly away from the staple.

With a loud tear, the rip went right up Katie's pant leg, nearly reaching her knee. "Well, now you're very in style, or whatever," Ashley commented, looking ruefully at Katie's ripped jeans.

Katie shrugged. "Come on, we'd better get back inside." Together, the girls stepped on the brick and grabbed hold of the window ledge. They pulled themselves up to the window—and found themselves face to face with Mr. Palmero.

5

Katie clasped her hands together nervously as she followed Ashley into the school office. "Hi, Ms. Trencher," Ashley cheerily greeted the skinny, sour-looking school secretary.

A pinched smile formed on Ms. Trencher's thin red lips. "Here to see Mr. Marshall again?" she inquired.

Ashley pouted piteously. "I'm afraid so. My friend Katie and I were the victims of a cruel prank, resulting in an unfortunate misunderstanding."

Katie blinked when Ashley described her as her "friend." They really weren't friends, but somehow she appreciated Ashley saying they were.

"Unfortunate misunderstandings seem to dog your heels, don't they, Ms. Kingsley," Ms. Trencher observed wryly.

Ashley nodded sadly, ignoring the obvious irony in Ms. Trencher's tone. "I must have been born under an unlucky star," Ashley said.

"Oh, is that it? I see," said Ms. Trencher. "Well, have a

seat, girls. Mr. Marshall will see you when he's free."

"When will that be?" Ashley asked boldly.

Ms. Trencher's eyes narrowed with annoyance. "Do you have a prior engagement, Ms. Kingsley, a more pressing appointment, perhaps?"

"No," Ashley replied. "I was just wondering."

"Mr. Marshall will see you when he finds a moment in his schedule," Ms. Trencher said stiffly.

Ashley seemed completely unaffected by Ms. Trencher's icy tone. She smiled charmingly at her. "Thank you."

Ms. Trencher went back to typing on her purring electric typewriter as Katie and Ashley waited, sitting on two of the worn leather chairs against the wall. "When he *finds* a moment in his schedule," Ashley mimicked Ms. Trencher under her breath. "Give me a break. Like he's *so* busy."

"What do you think he'll do?" Katie asked Ashley.

"Oh, nothing," Ashley scoffed. "I've got old Marshall right where I want him. He loves me."

"He does?" Katie asked, bewildered. "Are you here a lot?"

"You could say that," Ashley admitted. As she spoke, Ashley examined one of her perfectly manicured oval nails and rubbed an invisible speck on the cuticle of her delicate thumb. "Do you believe that idiot Darrin didn't even get in trouble?"

"He wasn't out the window," Katie reminded her.

Katie was a little surprised at Ashley's impeccable manicure. In Katie's experience, girls with nails like Ashley's were conceited, stuck-up little Miss Prisses.

Hardly the type of girl to go sailing out a first-floor window to help a near-total stranger.

Ashley's careful nails didn't match her reckless-looking, wild red hair, either. But now that Katie had a chance to get a good look at Ashley, she could see that Ashley's concern for her appearance didn't end at her fingertips. Her jeans had a sharply ironed crease. Her white cotton shirt with its tiny edge of lace at the collar was still so snowy and flat, it had to be starched. The colorful, thick cotton cardigan she wore had an artistic knit-in design of a sunset over a mountaintop. Unlike Katie's frayed hightops, Ashley's ankle boots weren't scuffed at all. In fact, they shone slightly, as if they'd been recently polished.

Next to Ashley, Katie suddenly felt messy in her faded jeans and blue Pearl Jam sweatshirt. The tear in her jeans didn't help, either. She looked down at her own large hands with their clipped short nails and compared them with Ashley's impossibly graceful fingers.

Katie had just never been that interested in fashion. And she sure didn't have the patience to fuss with her nails, hair, or makeup. She was who she was, and Ashley seemed to like her anyway.

Katie could be generous, too, she decided. She was willing to overlook Ashley's incredibly well-groomed appearance. So far she was shaping up as just the opposite of all Katie's fixed ideas about self-centered airheads who only thought about hair, makeup, and boys. Katie sensed that Ashley might be someone Katie would like to know better.

"Darrin's really got it bad for you," Ashley said after a moment.

"What?" Katie yelped.

Ms. Trencher looked up sharply, and Katie shot her a quick, apologetic smile.

Ashley smiled. "Can't you tell? He just bugs you because he likes you. He's very immature like that."

"Oh, pul-lease," Katie moaned. "Give me a break."

Ashley smiled. "I know what you mean. Can you picture yourself on a date with Darrin?"

"Oh, yuk," said Katie.

"Mr. Marshall will see you now," said Ms. Trencher.

"Don't worry about anything," Ashley said under her breath as they got up. "Let me do the talking, okay?"

"Sure," Katie agreed fervently. *I haven't even been here six weeks and I've already landed in the principal's office,* she thought sadly.

They stepped past Ms. Trencher's desk into a small, narrow office. Mr. Marshall sat at his desk by the window. He was a tall man with wispy blond hair; large, pale blue eyes; and a fat belly. "Hello, Ms. Kingsley. What seems to be the problem today?" he greeted Ashley.

"No problem, not really," said Ashley, helping herself to a seat at the table in the middle of the room. "This is Katie Nelson, she's new here in Pine Ridge, and all she was trying to do was find a home for some sweet little kittens. But this kid in our homeroom, who shall remain nameless since he's such a creep, threw her photo of the kittens out the window. Well, Katie just has to find homes for the kittens fast. You know how it is with kittens. They get drowned or gassed—or worse. So she had to think fast. Innocent lives were at stake. Without any concern for herself, she leapt out the window after the photo, and injured herself terribly."

Ashley turned to Katie. "Show him your leg."

Katie lifted her leg so he could see the tear in her jeans.

"Did you cut yourself?" Mr. Marshall asked.

"No," Ashley answered for Katie. "But it hurt dreadfully at the time, I'm sure. Anyway, I went out the window to help her, but when Mr. Palmero came in, he tragically misunderstood the entire situation and sent us down to see you."

Mr. Marshall took them in with his light blue eyes. "How did Mr. Palmero misunderstand the situation?"

"He thought we were just goofing around, trying to be funny, when nothing could have been further from the truth," Ashley explained with a tone of wounded dignity.

"Under no circumstances should you girls ever climb out the window again," Mr. Marshall said levelly.

"Oh, we know that," said Ashley. "We just lost our heads completely."

"Try to keep hold of them in the future," Mr. Marshall replied.

"Oh, we absolutely will," Ashley assured him.

"Ms. Nelson?" Mr. Marshall inquired.

"No, sir, I won't jump out the window ever again," Katie replied.

"See that you don't," said Mr. Marshall firmly, yet with the quickest flicker of a smile.

"Hey, Mr. Marshall, want a kitten?" Ashley asked.

Katie stared at Ashley in disbelief. In her old school,

if you got sent to the principal, you got out of there as fast as possible. Ashley was definitely pressing her luck.

"I might," said Mr. Marshall.

Surprised, Katie took the photo from her back pocket and shyly slid it across the table to Mr. Marshall.

"Cute," he said, looking at the photo. "My kids have been begging for kittens. Do you have two left?"

"Two?" Katie gasped. "Absolutely. They can't leave their mother for about a month or so, but just tell me which two you want, and they're yours."

Mr. Marshall picked a black kitten and a gray tiger-striped one and then sent Katie and Ashley back to class.

"You're amazing!" laughed Katie when they were out in the hall. "I thought we'd have detention, for sure. And you even found homes for two of the kittens!"

Ashley smiled. "Nothing to it. We didn't do anything so terrible. That's why Mr. Marshall is always glad to see me—I'm easy to deal with. Last time I was in to see him was just because I put an iguana in Ms. Fisher's desk drawer."

"An iguana?" Katie exclaimed. "Where did you find an iguana?"

"He belongs to my brother Jeremy."

"Why did you put it in Ms. Fisher's desk?"

"Because a bunch of us didn't think it was right to kill frogs and dissect them in lab. So we refused, and she assigned us a massive report on the workings of the human body instead. It was much harder than dissecting the frog. She just did it because she was mad at us for standing up for the frogs. So this was sort of like the revenge of green, bumpy life-forms. You should have seen her when she opened her drawer. She jumped up, knocked over her chair, and went all pale. It was really funny."

"How did she find out you put it there?" Katie asked.

"She was going to punish the whole class, so I had to admit it. It was no biggie." Ashley shook her head and laughed at the memory of the event. "Hey, you know, I'd kind of like a kitten. Do you think I could have one?"

"Sure," Katie agreed readily as they began walking down the hall together. "Don't you, uh, have to check with your parents or anything?"

"Nah, we have so many animals on the ranch that they wouldn't even notice another one."

"The ranch?" Katie asked. "You live on a ranch?"

"Yeah, the Pine Manor Horse Ranch. It's a horse farm. Do you ride?"

"I took a few lessons at summer camp once," Katie said.

"You should come home with me sometime. We can go riding together if it's not too cold. There are great trails by the ranch."

"That would be great," Katie said enthusiastically. Just before . . . the accident, Katie's parents had agreed to horseback riding lessons. But the way Uncle Jeff complained about bills, she could just imagine asking for riding lessons now. He already resented the fact that he even had to feed her.

Katie remembered the conversation she'd overheard the other evening between her aunt and uncle. A cold emptiness swept through her at the memory. They didn't want her there. No one did.

What was the use of making any friends here? People always disappointed you. They either went away for a weekend and never returned, or hated you because it cost money to feed you. Or forgot about you as soon as you left town, like Addy seemed to have.

"What's wrong?" Ashley asked. "You got a sad look on your face all of a sudden."

Katie looked at Ashley's concerned face and the empty hole inside her seemed a little smaller, less empty, somehow. It might be nice to have a friend. They didn't have to be best friends. But it would be good to have someone to do things with. "Oh, I was just thinking of something. It's nothing, really," she told Ashley. "When would it be good for me to come over?"

"How about today?" Ashley suggested.

"Today?" said Katie. "Well . . . sure. Why not?"

To her amazement, Katie felt a terrific happiness soar up inside her.

"Great," said Ashley. "You can take my bus home with me."

"Great!" Katie echoed her happily. Who could tell? Maybe they really would get to be friends. The idea made Katie feel so good that it embarrassed her. She didn't want Ashley to think she was desperate for a friend or anything like that.

She forced the smile from her lips.

"We'd better get to class," Katie said seriously.

"I guess so," said Ashley. "Let's go."

6

I had a dream the other night. I dreamed I was traveling around the country with a friend.

Katie put her pen down and peeked up at her study-hall teacher. She seemed intent on the papers she was correcting. She wouldn't care whether Katie was actually doing schoolwork or writing in her journal.

Katie went back to writing in the marble-covered journal she'd brought to school with her.

I couldn't see the friend's face. I don't think it was Addy. But I had the feeling that I liked this friend very much. It was just the two of us. Kind of like hobos. Only it was really fun. In my dream, we were somewhere warm and went swimming in a stream. When we got back to our blanket, milkshakes and hamburgers were waiting for us. We just ate them, not knowing or caring where they came from.

I woke up from my dream in the middle of the night because Dizzy, Mel's mutt, was barking at something outside. But I didn't want to wake up because the dream was so great. I tried to go back to sleep and dream it again. When that didn't work, I just lay there thinking about what it would be like, sort of like having a waking dream.

Maybe some day I'll really do it. I wonder who the friend will be.

You know what I've been thinking? Lately I've been thinking it might be cool to be a writer. Don't ask me what I'd write about, because I have no idea. But something interesting is bound to happen to me sooner or later. If I take that trip, something interesting is sure to happen.

One thing I know for sure. If I stay here in Pine Ridge, nothing will ever happen at all. This has got to be the dullest place on earth!!! As soon as possible, I am leaving. Sometimes I picture myself turning into a clay statue. I picture the rain, wind, and the snow wearing me away little by little until nothing is left of me but a small, clay lump.

That's how I've been feeling lately. Like a small, clay lump.

I think being lonely has brought out a sort of mean, crabby side in my personality. I'm beginning to remind myself of some of those kids I used to see hanging on the corner near the high school. I understand now why they looked that way. That attitude keeps people away, so they don't mess with you. I know I'm trying to look like those kids on purpose so that people (people like my aunt, uncle, cousin, and kids like this super creep in my class named Darrin) won't mess with me. But deep down, I don't want to be like those kids who look so nasty and angry. I want to be the way I *was*. But I guess I'll never be the way I was, because nothing is ever going to be the way it was. Not ever again.

I understand those tough kids now. When you're around people who don't care about you, you feel like you have to stand up for yourself all the time. That's how I feel, and it gets to me.

Well, I don't want to be a downer. Here's something good. I'm going to this girl in my class's house. Her horse ranch, actually. I can't believe she really lives on a ranch! We might even ride if it's not too cold.

The way my luck has been going, the horse will probably kick me in the head or something.

7

"Get off the phone, would you, Aunt Rainie," Katie muttered at three o'clock that afternoon as she listened to the annoying *Beep! Beep! Beep!* of the busy signal. Disgusted, she hung up the pay phone in the school lobby. She'd been trying to reach Aunt Rainie all day to ask permission to go home with Ashley after school.

"Any luck?" asked Ashley, tossing back her coppery curls as she crossed the lobby toward Katie.

Katie shook her head. "It's probably hopeless. Once Aunt Rainie hits the phone in the afternoon, she doesn't get off for hours."

"Why don't you come home with me anyway? You can call her from my place," Ashley suggested.

Katie considered this a moment. She didn't want to get into trouble, but she *did* want to go to Ashley's. She wanted to go really badly. It would be great if she and Ashley could become friends. She'd been so lonely here in Pine Ridge. "I guess that would be all right," she agreed.

"Great," Ashley said with a happy smile. "Now we'd better run, or we'll miss my bus."

They raced down the hall and bolted out the back entrance just as the last kid was climbing onto Ashley's bus. Katie followed Ashley toward the back. As Katie slid into an empty back seat, Ashley started looking around as if she were trying to find someone.

Katie felt a sudden pang. *What if I'm in someone else's regular seat,* she worried. She followed Ashley's gaze until both their eyes rested on a slim, delicate girl with wavy white-blonde hair and large blue eyes who sat three seats ahead with another girl. "Good, Christina is probably doing a chart or whatever today, so she won't want to sit with me anyway," Ashley said.

Feeling relieved that she was in the clear, Katie settled back.

Christina turned around at the mention of her name and smiled at Ashley. "I think Ellen is a quadruple Cancer," she said excitedly.

"Is that bad?" asked the thin girl sitting next to Christina.

"Oh, no, not at all," said Christina passionately. "It's remarkable, though. It's so unusual to find someone with four planets in a row in the sign of Cancer, and I'm not even done with your chart yet. We may find more."

"Good luck," said Ashley good-naturedly as she sat beside Katie.

"What is she talking about?" Katie questioned.

"She's doing Ellen's horoscope chart," Ashley explained. "Christina knows everything about astrology. If you tell her the exact time and day you were born, she can figure out this whole big chart that tells you where all the planets were when you were born. It's supposed to tell you everything about yourself. You know, your true personality, or whatever."

"I don't believe that stuff. I don't even know my sign," said Katie. "I was thirteen November 17th. What does that make me?"

Ashley leaned up over her seat. "Katie's birthday was November 17th, Christina! What sign is that?"

"Scorpio," Christina called back. She turned and stared piercingly at Katie. "Scorpio is a great sign," she added emphatically. "It's very deep, very mystical. You are *so* lucky to be a Scorpio. It's one of my favorite signs." Christina's eyes glowed with enthusiasm as she spoke. Then she turned and went back to what she was doing.

"That's me, deep and mystical." Katie laughed scornfully.

Ashley shrugged. "Who knows? Maybe you really *are* deep and mystical."

"Yeah, right. Give me a break," said Katie, rolling her eyes.

Katie couldn't believe Ashley and Christina were really friends. Ashley seemed so cool, and Christina was an airy-fairy dizzbrain. Astrology! How could Ashley stand it? "Do you and Christina usually sit together on the bus?" asked Katie, carefully hiding her disbelief.

"Most of the time. She lives at the ranch, too."

"In the same house?"

"No, her mother works at the ranch. They have their own house. Christina may seem a little spacey at first, but she's cool," Ashley added. "Trust me."

"If you say so," said Katie, inwardly shaking her head. She didn't want to completely blow it with Ashley by telling her what she really thought. People who believed in junk like astrology were gullible and kind of pathetic—just like dumb little kids who thought they saw angels.

The bus ride to Pine Manor Ranch was almost twice as long as the ride Katie usually took home. Ashley, Christina, and Katie were the last ones on the bus when it finally rumbled up a bumpy hill. "Last stop," the bus driver called cheerfully as he stopped by a homey-looking red barn with a painted sign reading Pine Manor Ranch nailed to it.

When Christina stood, Katie saw she was tall and dressed in a heavy purple cape with silver stars embroidered along the collar. She pulled on a matching purple beret. At the front of the bus, she stopped to talk to the bus driver. "Albert," she said very seriously. "I wanted to remind you that today is the 16th."

The bus driver, a skinny, middle-aged man with almost no hair looked at her, perplexed. "So?"

"Remember we talked about 8 being a very favorable number for you," she said.

"Yeah," said Albert blankly. Then his eyes lit with understanding. "I get it! Sixteen, double 8's."

"Right," said Christina. "So if there was something you were thinking about doing, today is a very good day for you to do it."

"Christina is into numerology, too," Ashley explained as they moved up to the front of the bus.

"Thanks, Christina," said Albert. "I was going to

propose to my girlfriend. Maybe I'll do it tonight."

Christina touched his shoulder lightly. "Absolutely, Albert. You *must* do it tonight."

What a nut, thought Katie, studying Christina. Ashley must have just been trying to be polite, because to say Christina *seemed* spacey was the understatement of the century. *Seem,* nothing! She absolutely *was*!

Katie felt herself growing annoyed at Christina. Why did she have to be there to spoil things? Did she honestly believe all this crazy stuff about planets and numbers, or was it just a routine to get attention? Either way, Katie wanted no part of it—or her. She was obviously a real ditz.

Once they were off the bus, they passed a split-rail fence and walked down a wide dirt road. To their right, another split-rail fence outlined a rolling pasture where four horses—two glossy black stallions, and a white palomino spotted mare with a palomino colt—grazed contentedly. "How great! You're so lucky to live here," Katie blurted out.

"I guess," said Ashley. "I was born here, so it doesn't seem so special to me."

"It *is* special," Christina said confidently. "Mom says this place has very strong positive vibrations."

Katie rolled her eyes. "Strong what?"

"Vibrations. She says it's a very good place, with positive energy. She thinks there may be power spots in the woods behind the stables," Christina said.

"Power spots?" Katie questioned skeptically.

"Hey, would you need super-powered detergent to get out power spots?" Ashley teased.

"Or maybe you'd need Superman to come clean them," added Katie.

"Power spots are places in the world where—for some reason, no one knows why—cosmic energy is very strong," Christina explained earnestly. "They're places where spirits have an easy time crossing over from the other world."

"*What* other world?" Katie asked. Honestly, she knew what Christina meant. But for some reason she just felt like giving Christina a hard time.

"The spiritual world, of course," Christina answered, giving Katie a small scowl that deepened the color of her sky blue eyes. It wasn't a scowl of annoyance, though. It was more like the look of disappointment and pity a true believer gives to a skeptic.

Christina's eyes caught Katie by surprise. They were so deep and intense. And very focused. They *weren't* the eyes of a flaky airhead.

Katie looked away to avoid that earnest and steady gaze. "Oh, yeah, the spiritual world," she said, her voice rich with mockery. "That's where the ghosts live, right?"

In a flash of guilty memory, Katie suddenly remembered her experience in the woods when she'd thought she sensed her parents' spirits.

But that had just been a moment of weirdness, of wishful hoping. There hadn't really been anyone there.

Katie couldn't believe she'd been so dumb. She'd acted just like Christina, full of crazy fantasies. The fact that she'd ever acted like Christina the Flake embarrassed her. It made Christina even more annoying, like a living reminder of Katie's moment of weakness.

"Don't make fun of ghosts," said Christina. "I prefer to call them spirits."

"Ex*cuse* me?" Katie said. "I don't think the ghosts really care. They're dead. Remember?"

"Some people say the Pine Manor woods are haunted," Ashley jumped in. Her voice was a little high and overeager. Katie could tell she wanted to distract her from getting into an argument with Christina.

Then she remembered what Uncle Jeff had told her about the sign she'd found in the barn. The sign that came from the Pine Manor woods.

"Wait a minute! Are these the Pine Manor woods?" Katie asked excitedly.

"Yep," said Ashley. "Why?"

"Have you ever heard of the Angels Crossing Bridge?" Katie asked.

Ashley and Christina shook their heads. "I like the name, though," said Christina. "What is it?"

"I don't know. I found this old sign from there, and my uncle told me it came from a bridge in these woods," Katie explained.

"Angels Crossing," Christina murmured. "Just like spirits crossing over from the spiritual realm."

"Or like angels crossing the bridge," said Ashley. She laughed. "Or a deer crossing. Careful, angels crossing."

"That's what it made me think of, too," said Katie. "Want to go look for it?"

"The bridge?" asked Ashley.

Katie nodded. "Yeah. It might be kind of cool to see."

"We'd have to go pretty far into the woods," Ashley

said hesitantly. "I mean, I've been in most of the nearby woods, and I haven't ever seen a bridge."

Christina gazed at the crystal blue sky. "You only have a few hours of daylight left," she pointed out.

"We'll just look for a few hours then," Katie insisted.

"Would you rather do that than go riding?" Ashley asked.

"Kind of," said Katie. She wanted to ride, but she was excited to find the bridge. She wasn't sure why, but it was how she felt.

Still, she didn't want to seem weird. "I mean, we could ride. Whatever," she added, trying hard to sound casual.

"I wouldn't mind looking for the bridge," Ashley said. "I ride all the time. I'd rather do something different. Want to come, Christina?"

Say no, Katie silently urged her. She didn't want to hear all Christina's crazy talk about spirits, power spots, and astrology. She didn't need someone spouting all that nonsense, not when she might be having the best time she'd had since coming to Pine Ridge to live.

"Yes, it might be interesting," Christina agreed.

Katie's spirits sank. Oh, well, she'd just have to tune Christina out. She couldn't—she wouldn't—let a flake spoil her first good time in too long a time.

The dirt road wound past a small cabinlike house. "That's my house," said Christina. "I'm going to run inside and drop off my pack."

"Meet us behind the stable," Ashley told her.

Ashley and Katie continued down the dirt road until they came to a gray one-story ranch-style house with a long porch running along the front of it. "That's where we live," Ashley said. "Want to come in and put your pack inside?"

Katie stopped and stared at the house a minute. A wreath of pretty, dried flowers hung on the front door. A golden retriever with a shining coat lounged on the front porch. The house was neat and well cared for. They were nothing alike, yet it reminded Katie achingly of her old apartment on West 68th Street. Her mother had even had a similar dried wreath on their apartment door.

She couldn't bear to go inside.

"Would you bring it in for me?" Katie said quickly.

Ashley studied her a moment with a puzzled expression, but she didn't question her. "Okay."

"I, uh, want to go see the horses," Katie told her, just to give some sort of excuse for not coming in. "You don't mind, do you?"

Ashley smiled. "No. Go ahead."

"I'll meet you behind the stable, too," said Katie, not wanting to stand and stare at the tidy house. "Is that the stable over there?"

"Yeah," said Ashley, heading into the house. She pointed across the way to a long, low building. Its brown wooden siding gleamed in the slanting sunlight. "Go around back there."

Katie approached the building. There was a peaceful quiet about it. As she got to the door, she was already breathing the warm, musky smell of hay and horses. She nudged the door open. A horse snorted in his stable. Another whinnied softly. Soft brown eyes watched her impassively.

Katie shut the door and went behind the stable. She faced a thick wall of balsam, juniper, and Scotch pine trees. The rich, strong smell of pine forced the horsey smell from her nose.

The rustling pines seemed to call to her, speaking their own mysterious, compelling language.

She turned quickly at the approaching sound of light footsteps. Christina had changed from her long purple cape into a more casual—and more normal-looking— purple baseball jacket. The same purple beret as before perched rakishly on her head. Christina's pale skin glowed like marble in candlelight. Her long, classic nose was slightly flat at the end, and a small scar cut across one of her nearly invisible blonde eyebrows. Her extraordinary blue eyes seemed to miss nothing. Katie decided Christina was pretty in a willowy, exotic kind of way.

They stood side by side and gazed into the pines. Katie's mind wandered. She dropped her guard, lulled by the gently rustling branches. She wondered what the bridge would look like if they found it. She imagined luminous, wide-winged angels crossing it and remembered the time she thought she'd seen an angel when she was small.

"Do you believe in angels, Christina?" Katie asked softly.

The sound of her own voice was enough to snap Katie out of her dreamy state. Instantly, she wished she could call back her silly words.

Christina's blue eyes sparkled enthusiastically. "Yes, absolutely," Christina answered without hesitation.

How nice for you, thought Katie sincerely. She would

have liked to believe in angels, too. But she just couldn't. It was too . . . unbelievable.

"Do you?" Christina asked curiously.

Katie shook her head. Despite her memory of seeing her angel. Despite her feeling that her parents' spirits had been nearby. She didn't believe in any of that stuff. It was just imagination, just wishful thinking.

But, oh, how she longed to believe in angels and spirits—in a spiritual world. How she wished it could be true.

"Are you sure?" Christina asked.

"Sure I'm sure," Katie snapped at her irritably. "It's a nice idea. I almost wish I could. But no, I definitely don't believe in angels."

8

The moment Katie walked into the woods she felt
enveloped by the deep, deep quiet of the place. Her
footsteps, as well as those of Ashley and Christina, were
silenced by a thick carpet of fallen pine needles. Only
the whispering branches above them intruded on the
complete stillness.

The ancient trees formed a dense canopy over their
heads. Here and there, shafts of sharp white sunlight
fought their way through the trees. Katie glanced at a
sturdy young pine sapling standing in a shaft of light.
Lucky tree, she thought. Lucky to be born in a spot
where sunlight fell. In this place, there wasn't a lot of
sunlight to spare. And yet . . . it didn't feel gloomy at all.
If anything, Katie felt strangely energized.

Katie followed Ashley toward the right, where the
earth began to incline. Looking back, she realized
Christina wasn't with them. She was still back near the
edge of the woods. She stood with her eyes shut and
her arms out. "Come on, Christina!" Katie called.

Christina gave no indication that she heard Katie, so Katie ran back to her. "Come on," she repeated impatiently, shaking Christina lightly.

Christina's eyes fluttered open. "Oh, sorry. I wanted to see what it must feel like to be one of these trees."

Katie rolled her eyes. "Let's keep moving," said Katie, heading back up the hill.

"You know how I felt?" said Christina, walking behind her. "It felt ancient. This forest is very ancient. I felt it immediately. And I sensed a lot of life here—and not human life, either."

"Yeah, I'm sure you're right. There must be all kinds of life—chipmunks, squirrels, raccoons, foxes," said Katie as they caught up with Ashley.

"Not chipmunk life, intelligent life," Christina insisted.

"Hey! No dissing chipmunks," Ashley chided with a grin. "Remember Alvin? Of course Simon was the brainy one. But Alvin was smart, too." Ashley then began singing "Uptown Girl," in a voice like Alvin the Chipmunk's.

Katie laughed. Christina just shook her head good-naturedly. "Very funny," she said drily.

They climbed to the top of the hill and looked through the woods, which rose and fell gently. "There's supposed to be a haunted house on the other side of a creek," Ashley recalled. "Does anyone hear water?"

Katie listened. "No, but there's a little stream over there," she said, pointing. "Maybe it leads down to the creek."

"It might," Ashley agreed. They began following the stream through the woods. They trailed it up another hill and down its steep descent.

"Hey, what's that?" cried Katie as she spotted the peak of a green slate roof over the top of another hill.

"Let's see," said Ashley. The girls broke into a run, racing up the hill.

When they crested the hill, Katie stopped short. "That's no haunted house," she grumbled, disappointed. About fifteen yards ahead of them was a small, sunny clearing in the woods. In the center of it stood a run-down wooden shack with a boarded-over front door and windows. Its roof sagged in the middle, and its stone chimney was more than half tumbled down.

"What do you think it was?" Christina asked.

"Let's check it out," said Ashley, already heading toward it.

Katie ran along beside Ashley, soon passing her. She reached the house first. There was something business-like about its shape and lack of detail. It wasn't like a home, yet it was too small to have been a store or a hotel or office. It reminded Katie of the buildings in ghost towns in Western movies.

Breathless from running, Ashley joined Katie. "I bet I know what this is," she panted. "A long time ago, they used to do mining back here in these woods. This must be an old miner's shed, you know, where the men used to come out and rest and eat."

Katie stepped back and studied the house. "I bet you're right. I wonder what's inside." Three planks of old, splintered wood were nailed across the front door. Katie yanked on the middle one. With a brittle crack, it snapped in half, the rusted nails on the right side instantly pulling loose. "This will be a cinch to get into," Katie said, pleased.

"I wonder if it's safe," Ashley cautioned. "Maybe there's a bear or something in there."

"How could a bear get in if it's nailed shut?" Katie questioned skeptically.

"That's true," Ashley admitted. "But I still don't like the look of it. It looks sort of . . . I don't know . . . haunted."

"Oh, come on," Katie laughed.

"Well, it *is* old and rickety-looking," Ashley insisted. "What if the whole thing falls right on top of us?"

Katie began pulling on the second board. "I don't think it's going to . . ." Her voice trailed off as she turned to see what was making the thumping sound behind her.

Christina had stepped onto a wooden platform that sat just several inches above the ground about a yard to the left of the house. Her blonde hair tossed from side to side as she did a rhythmic, stomping sort of dance. As she moved, she repeated a chanting song in a language Katie didn't understand.

"What's she doing now?" Katie asked with a sigh.

Ashley frowned thoughtfully and watched a moment in puzzled silence. "Oh, I know!" she said. "She and her mother went to a bunch of Native American reservations last summer. She told me about this—it's a dance nomadic Indians did to honor the nature spirits each time they came to a new place."

Christina sensed them watching her and stopped dancing. "This platform is just like a natural ceremonial altar, isn't it?" she said, her eyes bright with enthusiasm.

"It's like it was just waiting here, waiting for someone to come along and use it to honor the spirits of this place."

"The spirits?" Katie yelped in disbelief. "There are spirits here?"

"Oh, yes," Christina said sincerely. "I feel their presence very strongly. This might even be a power spot."

Christina went back to her dance, twirling in a circle and letting her arms fly freely at her sides as she spun. Again, her voice rose in a loud, repetitive chant.

"No offense, Ashley, but your friend Christina is really off her—"

Katie's words were interrupted by Christina's high-pitched cry as she threw her head back and lifted her arms to the air.

I wish she'd shut up, thought Katie, shaking her head in dismay.

Suddenly, the ear-splitting pop of dry wood cracking pierced the air.

Katie looked over sharply.

The sound came from the platform. It seemed to, anyway. Christina didn't seem to have noticed it, though. She continued her dancing and chanting as if she were in her own world.

"Did you hear that sound?" Katie asked Ashley.

"I heard something coming from—" Ashley cut herself short as another loud, cracking sound came from the direction of the platform.

Katie looked over at Christina. Her blonde hair flew as she threw her head back and raised her arms into the air. Then, suddenly, Christina disappeared, as if the earth had opened up and swallowed her whole.

9

"Oh, no!" cried Ashley, her hands flying to her face.

Where the platform—and Christina—had been a moment before was a gaping hole. Shards and splinters of wood spiked its edges.

The horrible cracking sound still seemed to ring in the still forest air as Katie knelt at the edge. All she could see below was steady, unrelieved blackness.

"Christina!" she yelled frantically down the hole. No answer came.

Katie looked up at Ashley, her eyes wide with fear. "It's pitch black down there. I can't see her." *I can't hear her, either,* she added silently. *And that's even worse.*

"I wonder if this is a mining shaft," Ashley said, getting to her knees and cautiously creeping out onto what was left of the platform.

"It must be," Katie said, desperately trying to remember anything she might ever have known about mining shafts. How deep were they? Did they have ladders? Was there water in them? She was starting to feel panicky.

"Christina!" she shouted frantically into the hole once again. "Are you okay?"

This time, her call was answered by a low, moaning sound. "I'm . . . okay, I think. But I can't move," Christina's voice floated faintly up the shaft.

"She can't move!" Ashley gasped. "Oh, Katie, what are we going to do? It'll be dark soon!" she cried, looking at the sky.

Katie lowered herself onto her stomach and crept closer to the hole. She peered down. Now that her eyes had adjusted to the murk, she guessed that the hole was about twelve feet deep. Its dirt walls were crisscrossed with heavy, wooden beams. There was no ladder.

Katie could see Christina's legs below in a tiny patch of faded sunlight. The rest of her was shrouded in shadow. "Can you move anything?" she called down.

"I . . . I guess so," Christina said shakily. "But my arms . . . my arms. I can't move them. My right arm hurts so much."

"Her arms are broken," Ashley said. Her freckles stood out sharply on her paper white face.

"We've got to get her out of there. I wonder if there's a rope or something in that shed," Katie said. "You wait here. I'll go check."

"All right," Ashley agreed. "Hurry."

Katie ran back to the mining shed and began yanking on the remaining boards covering the door. "All right!" she cheered as the last board finally ripped loose.

Katie tried the rusted doorknob. With a creak, the door opened. She stepped into a musty room with dirty gray walls and plain plank floor. If you didn't count cobwebs, it was completely empty. Disappointed, Katie was about to leave when she spotted a narrow, half-open closet. She swung it open, and there—like an answer to a prayer—sat a coil of rope.

Katie snapped it up and hurried outside. In the daylight, she saw that the dirty white rope was badly frayed in many spots. She realized that that was probably why it had been left behind when everything else was taken. Well, it was all they had. She'd just have to hope it would hold.

"Make a loop and a slipknot," called Ashley, who was now up on her knees beside the pit opening.

Katie kept hold of one end and tossed the other end of the rope to her. "You'll have to do it. I don't know how."

Ashley caught the rope and deftly looped it, working the ends into a sliding knot. "We use this kind of loop with the horses," she explained as she worked.

When Ashley finished tying the loop, she tossed it down into the hole. "Put it around your waist, Christina," she called. "We'll pull you up."

"I can't," came Christina's faint reply. "My arms!"

Katie noticed that a cold wind had picked up in the past few minutes. It tossed her hair and blew down her neck. She pulled up the collar of her jacket and took her crumpled baseball cap from her pocket. As she tugged it on, she looked up at the sky. The first dusty pink streaks of sunset had invaded the hazy blue.

Ashley and Katie crawled to the edge of the hole and peered down. The shifting light now made half of Christina visible. Katie cringed at the sight of her right arm. Even though it was covered by the sleeve of her jacket, Katie could see it was bent in a strange, unnatural way. "Her arm is definitely broken," she said to Ashley. "Christina," she called down. "Can you wiggle into the rope without using your arms?"

"I can't," Christina wailed.

Katie could tell she was beginning to panic.

"Don't worry, Christina, we're going to get you out," she said soothingly. "It's gonna be okay."

Ashley bit her lower lip to stop its trembling. She, too, could see Christina's terribly twisted right arm.

"Christina, I can see that you've hurt your right arm," Katie called carefully. "Is your other arm okay?"

"I can't move it," Christina quavered. "It . . . it doesn't hurt like the other one, but I can't move it."

"I'll have to go down and help her," said Ashley.

Katie knew she was right. "I'll go," she offered.

"No, you stay here and pull us up."

Katie nodded. She was taller and larger than Ashley. It made sense for her to be the one to do the pulling. "The rope has a lot of frayed spots," she pointed out to Ashley.

Ashley examined the rope and frowned. "It's pretty bad, isn't it? Well, we'll just have to keep our fingers crossed."

Katie stood back about three feet away from the platform. She spread her legs for a steady stance, then wrapped the rope around her waist twice and gripped it with both hands. "Ready," she said to Ashley.

Ashley set her lips together tightly in an expression both worried and yet determined. Gripping the rope, she sat at the end of broken wood. Slowly, carefully, she turned around and let herself drop down into the hole.

As Ashley's shoulders disappeared beneath the hole, Katie staggered, pulled forward by Ashley's weight. "Whoa!" she heard Ashley cry out.

"It's all right. I've got you," Katie called, surprised by how hard it was to keep herself from being yanked into the hole. She leaned back to counterbalance Ashley's weight.

"Don't snap. Hold tight. Just don't snap," Katie muttered to the rope as if it were a living thing. Suddenly, Katie felt the tension on the rope ease.

"I'm down!" Ashley called. "Christina's arm is stuck on something. It's just her jacket. The arm seems okay."

Katie ran to the hole and looked down. Ashley was working intently to free Christina's left sleeve. Christina gazed up at Katie with a drawn, pale face and tried to smile.

This time, Katie noticed a wooden door. It seemed to be built right into the dirt wall. "Ashley, try that door," she suggested. "Maybe there's something inside that might help."

Ashley stopped working on Christina's sleeve and got to her feet. She pulled on the door's rusted handle. It wouldn't budge. "No good," she called up to Katie.

"All right," said Katie. "It was worth a try."

Ashley went back to trying to free Christina's sleeve. "This isn't going to work," she said with a defeated sigh. "Her sleeve is caught on a jagged piece of wood sticking out of the floor. Christina, I'm going to have to take off your jacket."

Slowly Ashley tried to help Christina out of her jacket. Katie could see how much Christina was favoring her broken arm. It made even getting the left arm out a slow process. Ashley worked gingerly but doggedly. At last, Christina's left arm was free.

"Christina, I'm going to try to move your other arm, okay?" she said gently. Even with all her care, Ashley couldn't avoid hurting Christina.

She winced in pain when Ashley touched her arm. "Ow! Ow! Ow!" she cried out as Ashley peeled back the sleeve.

"You'll be out soon, Christina," Katie called down. "Just hang in there a little longer." When the jacket was completely off, Ashley fitted the looped rope around Christina's waist.

"She's ready to go," Ashley called up to Katie. "I'll push her up as far as I can, then you pull her the rest of the way."

"Okay." Katie stepped back and took a firm hold of the rope. "Ready!" she called. Instantly, she felt Christina's weight on the rope. Her hands burned as the rope pulled. Pulling Christina up was much harder than lowering Ashley had been. Katie blew air into her cheeks, puffing them up with the effort of pulling.

Then, suddenly, Christina seemed much heavier. "I can't reach to push her up anymore," Ashley called. Christina's entire weight was now at the other end of the rope.

Katie clenched her teeth together. She couldn't let go now. She had to hold on no matter what.

Then . . . *snap!*

Katie flew backward and fell to the ground, landing hard.

Christina screamed.

Katie heard a terrible thud and a loud groan.

The short end of the rope lay by Katie's side. Quickly, Katie scrambled to the platform and crawled out to the hole. Ashley lay on the ground next to Christina, who sat with tears running down her cheeks.

Cold terror ran through Katie. "Is Ashley breathing?" she called to Christina.

Christina nodded. "But she hit her head hard when we fell."

"Can you throw me the rope?"

Christina struggled to her knees, then staggered to her feet. With her left hand, she tossed the rope toward Katie.

Katie stretched into the hole as far as she could reach. The rope kept falling short of her grasp. "It's no use," she said. "I'm going to get help."

She pulled off her jacket. As she did, she remembered her lighter was still in her pocket. She took it out, then tossed the jacket into the hole. The cold bit into her but she tried to ignore it.

"You'll freeze," Christina objected as the jacket fell on her.

"You guys need it more," said Katie. "I can keep moving. And I have my lighter."

"You shouldn't smoke," said Christina.

Katie rolled her eyes. "Thanks for the advice. Listen, I'll be back fast. Don't worry, okay?"

"Okay," Christina said. "I'll chant for help from the spirits."

"Yeah, you do that," said Katie quickly. "Good idea." *If chanting kept Christina's mind off her pain and the scary predicament she was in, it probably was a good idea*, Katie thought.

Katie took off, running at full tilt back up the hill they'd come down. In the pines, it was darker than in the clearing. The dying light of twilight made it even more difficult to see. *The stream*, Katie reminded herself. They'd followed the stream in, and she could follow it back out.

Her eyes scanned the ground until she detected a glistening of light. Sure enough, it was the stream. She ran alongside it, following it for almost fifteen minutes until it forked off into two separate veins.

Katie stopped and gazed around the dark woods. Which was the right way? She didn't remember the stream branching like this. Had she already passed the spot where they first picked up the stream's trail? She wasn't sure.

She shivered violently as a blast of wind swept past her. She wondered how Christina and Ashley were doing there in that dark, cold mining shaft. One thing was for sure, she had to keep moving—or all three of them would freeze.

Katie picked the branch of the stream she thought looked most likely to be the right one and continued to follow it. It was hard to know if she was going in the right direction. The shifting shadows made everything look different. Was she walking out of the woods or further into them?

Katie hugged herself for warmth. She bit her lip to

stop her teeth from chattering.

This was hopeless. She was lost. She'd let them all down.

Rubbing her hands together for warmth, Katie fought back her tears. For some strange reason she suddenly heard her mother's voice in her head. *Hi! Hi! My Angel Pie.* Her mother used to say that to her when she came home from school. When Katie was in the sixth grade, she'd asked her mother to stop saying it. It was so babyish. Too embarrassing. But her mother had insisted on whispering it anyway. And, secretly, Katie had really liked it when she did.

One hot tear escaped from Katie's eye and rolled down her frozen cheek. "Hi! Hi! My Angel Pie," she spoke out loud. "Hi! Hi! My . . ." Her voice choked in her throat at the memory.

Katie covered her eyes with her hands to stop the tears. Her entire body shook with sadness and cold.

Suddenly, though, Katie looked up. She cocked her head and listened. What was that sound? Was it a motor? Traffic on a roadway? It was coming from the other side of a hill off to her right.

Wiping her face, she headed toward the hill. As she got closer, she realized it was a steady noise, not an animal or the wind.

At the top of the hill, she looked down and saw a wide creek at the bottom. This was the source of the sound as its rushing water burbled noisily over and around the rocks and boulders in its path. Pink and yellow lights from the setting sun glinted here and there like faint jewels.

Beautiful as it was, Katie shook her head forlornly. They had definitely not passed this creek on the way in. She was way off course.

Yet . . . maybe the creek would lead her somewhere. Following it was worth a try, anyway.

Katie stepped down the hill toward the creek. After that, everything happened in a fast jumble. Her foot slid on a muddy spot and shot out from under her. She felt herself tumble forward and bang her head on a rock.

She grabbed wildly for something to hold onto, but there was nothing. She was sliding, sliding, sliding down the steep hill toward the creek.

10

Katie opened her eyes and was instantly blinded by light. She blinked and tried to figure out where she was. Turning her head away from the light, she realized she was lying on a wooden floor. Her head was cushioned by a rolled cloth of some kind. A heavy army blanket had been placed over her.

As her eyes adjusted, she saw that she was lying inside an old-fashioned covered bridge. The blinding light shone from a hurricane lantern suspended on a crossbeam from the inside of the bridge's roof.

Squinting, Katie could see three people with her inside the bridge, two women and one man, all about nineteen or twenty. They were intently playing cards, sitting on wooden chairs around a small, square table covered by a red-checked cloth.

Katie leaned up on her elbows to get a better look at this odd sight. They were so engrossed in their card game that they didn't seem to notice her.

Narrowing her eyes to block out the glare from the

hurricane lantern seemed to work. Katie studied the three. There was definitely something strange about them. It was their clothing, she realized. It looked as old-fashioned as the bridge itself, as if they'd stepped out of one of the old black-and-white movies her parents used to like to watch on TV late at night.

One of the women, the one directly facing Katie, had beautiful, delicate features and flawless, glowing skin. She looked like a model or an actress. Her blonde hair glistened in soft waves around her face and was pulled back at the nape of her neck. She wore a fitted blue chiffon dress with gently ruffled sleeves.

The young man to her right put a playing card down in the center of the table and smiled. "Beat that, if you can," he challenged the women good-naturedly. He wore wide trousers and suspenders over a loose-fitting white shirt and saddle shoes. His suit jacket was draped over the back of his chair. On his head was a wide-brimmed fedora, pushed casually back off his forehead. A shock of reddish hair tumbled down onto his broad brow.

The woman on the left had jet black hair pulled back tightly into a bun. Her features were sharp, angular, strikingly beautiful. She wore a soft purple suit jacket with matching wide pants.

Suddenly, Katie noticed another unusual thing about them. Their eyes were all the same color—a weird, unearthly shade of violet blue she'd never seen before on anyone else.

Katie jumped slightly as the man turned unexpectedly toward her. "She's awake," he announced to the others, his kind, lively face breaking into a wide grin. "How do you feel, Katie?" he asked pleasantly.

"All right, I guess," Katie answered haltingly. "How . . . How did you know my name?"

"Good guess," the man said with an offhand shrug.

Excellent guess, thought Katie suspiciously. *Too good.*

The sophisticated-looking woman with the black hair leaned forward in her chair. "Are you cold?" she asked Katie.

"Not too bad," said Katie honestly. The blanket they'd covered her with was incredibly warm. "Aren't *you* cold?" She realized they weren't dressed for the cold at all. They didn't even have jackets.

"It's pretty warm in here," the black-haired woman said.

"The cold doesn't bother us, anyway," said the beautiful blonde woman, her voice ending in a lilting laugh.

"Edwina," scolded the other woman.

"What?" Edwina asked, wide-eyed at the reproach. "Is it a secret? Nobody told *me* it was."

"I don't know," said the other woman. "No one told us it *wasn't* a secret. I just *assumed* it was a secret."

"Well *I* assumed it wasn't," insisted Edwina huffily.

"What are you talking about?" Katie wondered out loud.

The man stood and gestured toward the women. "These are my sisters, Edwina and Norma Galen," he introduced them. "And I'm Ned Galen."

"Hi. I'm Katie, but I guess you already know that. Your names? Is that the secret? Or is it a secret that you're related? No, it couldn't be. Anyone could tell that from looking at your eyes."

"Our eyes?" asked Ned.

"They're exactly the same!" said Katie, hardly able to believe he didn't know that. "So that couldn't be the secret. What's the secret?"

Ned turned to his sisters as if looking to them for the answer. "Uh . . ."

Our names," said Norma. "That's the secret. We're the Galens and . . . we're spies . . . for this country, of course . . . good spies . . . but, still, we have to keep our identities a secret. You can understand that, can't you?"

Katie nodded slowly. If they were spies it explained how they knew her name. Maybe. Spies usually knew unusual things. Still, why weren't they cold?

"Now, Norma," Ned chided gently. "We should not be telling lies, *especially* not us."

"But Ned, I really think we're not supposed to . . . you know," Norma insisted.

"I think it's a little late now," Edwina said as she gathered the cards into a pile.

"Oh, all right," Norma grumbled. "Tell her. But I still say we're not supposed to."

Ned faced Katie and smiled warmly. "We're angels."

"Yeah! Right!" Katie scoffed. "And I'm Glinda, the Good Witch of the North. Tell me another one."

Edwina came around to Katie and bent down to her when she spoke. "We heard you call out for an angel. Didn't you?"

"No, that wasn't her," said Norma. "It was her friend."

"No, her friend was chanting for spirits," Edwina said.

Edwina's words made Katie sit up alertly. How did she know Christina had been chanting?

"Well . . ." Norma shot back pointedly, her eyebrows raised. "Aren't we . . . you know."

"It's not the same thing," insisted Edwina.

"It counts as the same as far as I'm concerned," said Norma. "If what Katie said counts, then chanting for spirits counts."

"What did I say?" Katie questioned.

"You know," said Edwina kindly. "The 'Hi! Hi!' thing."

"Hi! Hi! My Angel Pie," Katie repeated, totally bewildered.

Norma snorted derisively. "Sure. Like that's a real call for help. It doesn't qualify under rule number five."

"Rule five?" Katie questioned. These people were out there, all right.

"Rule number five: The recipient of aid must make a deliberate mental or verbal request," Norma recited.

"It does so qualify," said Edwina. "Everyone asks in their own way." She brushed Katie's bangs away from her forehead. Her touch was warm and feathery soft. "Oh, dear, you really whacked your head hard. It's going to be black and blue, I'm afraid. When we found you by the creek, you were pale as a . . . well, quite pale. It was lucky you called us when you did."

Norma stood up abruptly. "The chanting is fading. I can hardly hear it. Katie's awake now, which was what we were waiting for. We'd better do something quickly."

The chanting! "That's Christina," said Katie quickly. "We've got to get help for her. She and Ashley have fallen into a mine shaft, and they're both hurt. But I'm not even sure of the way back now."

Ned held out a fist and uncurled his fingers to reveal a small old-fashioned compass with a gleaming gold rim. "Have no fear. Ned the Woodsman is here. Can you tell me anything about the location of your friends?"

"They fell into a mine shaft near an old mining shed. I was coming for help, but I got lost. I've never been in these woods before, and I have no idea where anything is. If you could just get me out of the woods, I could get help from people who know their way around," Katie told him.

"Well, yes, that might be the best course of action," Ned agreed. "All right, let's go."

Ned stood on a chair and unhooked the lantern from the beam. Edwina reached out and took Katie's hand. Katie got up, feeling stiff. The bruise on her head ached, but otherwise she didn't feel seriously hurt.

"Who are you guys, really?" she asked. She hated having to rely on such weird people for help, but they seemed okay enough, despite their strangeness. Anyway, they were Katie's only hope.

"Don't worry about that now," Edwina said. "We'd better find help for your friends."

Katie followed them out of the bridge and into the night. Looking behind, she saw the bridge, which spanned the creek. Moonlight glanced off its peaked roof and sparkled on the rushing water below it. "Is that the Angels Crossing Bridge?" she asked.

Norma nodded.

"What were you all doing there?" Katie asked as they

followed Ned, who led the way through the woods with the lantern.

"We were playing cards," Edwina replied. "Hey, I bet you think we were playing bridge. Get it? *Bridge?*"

"What game were you playing?" Katie asked, to be polite.

"Hearts," said Norma seriously.

They walked together in the darkness while Katie thought about her strange companions. They couldn't really be angels. Where were their wings? Their halos? Besides, she didn't even believe in angels! And *Norma*, *Edwina*, and *Ned* didn't sound like angel names!

"How are you doing?" Ned asked, looking over his shoulder at her.

"Okay," She replied. "Hey, if you're really an angel, how come you don't have a name like *Gabriel* or something? What kind of name is *Ned* for an angel?"

"*Gabriel* is more of an archangel name," Ned replied. "We're just plain angels—worker angels. Archangels do the big, important work—carrying inspirational messages of peace to presidents and compassionate wisdom to generals, like that. We take care of regular people and the more day-to-day type of problems."

"Oh," said Katie. Was she really having this conversation? Was Ned for real? It was all so weird, and yet these three seemed to believe what they were saying.

"What's wrong with the name *Ned*, anyway?" asked Ned, sounding mildly insulted.

"Well," said Katie. "I never met anyone named *Ned* before. They only person I ever heard of named *Ned* was Ned Nickerson, Nancy Drew's boyfriend."

"Is Nancy Drew a friend of yours?" Ned asked.

Katie looked at him quizzically. How could anyone not know who Nancy Drew was? Maybe it was because he was a guy.

"Nancy Drew is a detective in a book series," Katie explained. "Your sisters know who she is."

She looked to Edwina and Norma for confirmation on this point. They simply shook their heads, their expressions slightly apologetic.

"Everyone knows Nancy Drew," said Katie. "The first Nancy Drew books came out way back in the 1930s!"

"Way *back* in the thirties?" Ned questioned, starting to look worried.

Edwina took Katie's arms gently. She wore a pained expression. "You mean this isn't the . . ."

"I told you it wasn't the 1930s!" Norma said, obviously annoyed. "I told you both, but would you listen?"

"Wait a minute!" Katie cried. "What are you guys talking about?"

"Oh, nothing," said Norma with a sweet smile.

In the lantern light, Katie saw Norma look sharply at Edwina. Edwina cringed slightly. "What year *is* this?" she asked gingerly.

Katie told her the year.

"I was so sure it was 1933," Edwina said meekly.

Katie's brow furrowed with confusion. How could Edwina think it was 1933? Come to think of it, though, they *did* sort of look like they would have fit right into that time. Katie remembered pictures of her grandparents from the thirties, and these three looked as if they'd stepped right out of some of those faded old photos.

Ned laughed. "So, uh, how do we look for the nineties?"

"Kind of weird," Katie answered honestly. Then, to soften the blow, she added, "You know, kind of old-fashioned." As they walked, Katie found it difficult to keep pace with Ned's brisk pace. She fell back between Edwina and Norma, who walked side-by-side deep in conversation. Whatever was going on here, it was obvious to Katie that these guys were totally into it.

"And I'll bet *our* names don't fit in, either," Katie heard Norma whisper irritably to Edwina. "Some big idea *you* had—check the 1933 birth registry," she scoffed.

"I guess I read the schedule wrong," Edwina said whispered back apologetically. "Maybe we can change them."

"We can't change our names once we've registered them," Norma hissed. "You know that! We're stuck with these names."

"Are you all right, Katie?" Ned called over his shoulder.

Katie hurried to catch up with him. "Yeah, I think so."

Ned smiled at her and took off his fedora. When his hat was off, Katie noticed for the first time that he had shoulder-length hair tucked behind his ears. Funny. She hadn't realized it before. *It must have been hidden down the collar of his shirt,* she decided.

They continued walking through the deep woods. The moonlight was blocked by the trees, leaving Ned's lantern their only light. Katie saw only blackness around her. Yet, strangely, she wasn't cold. The temperature had changed drastically since the time she fell down to the creek.

Ned checked his compass. "This way," he said. Katie realized that he'd taken off his jacket. In the lantern light she saw that his shirt was now untucked, and it had colorful Mexican embroidery down the front. Strange that she hadn't noticed that before.

They followed Ned for another five minutes. Katie noticed that Norma's hair now hung in two long braids. She looked to Edwina and saw that her wavy, golden hair was now undone completely and fell to her waist.

Their hair must have come undone while we walked, she thought.

"How are you feeling?" Edwina asked kindly. "How's your head?"

"It kind of aches," Katie told her. As she spoke, it seemed to her that Edwina's dress had changed somehow. It was now a flowing and ruffled peasant dress. "Did you have a different dress on before?" Katie asked her.

"Do you like this?" Edwina asked, spreading the narrow, crinkled pleats wide for the full effect. "It *is* sort of pretty, isn't it?"

"Yeah, but, isn't it a different dress from—"

"Here we are," Ned interrupted.

Katie gazed around. They were still in the middle of the woods in total blackness. What was he talking about? "We're not anywhere!" she cried.

Ned brushed a thick layer of pine needles away with his hands. Katie was surprised to see that he was wearing sandals. Sandals! Had he been wearing them before?

As he brushed away the pine, needles, a wooden hatch in the ground was revealed. "Ta da!" Ned sang out gleefully. He bent and tugged on a curved iron handle, easily lifting the hatch door.

Katie peered down into a pitch black hole.

"Down we go," said Ned cheerfully.

11

"I'm not going down there," said Katie, backing away. "What is that?"

"It's the best way to help your friends," said Norma. Katie stared hard at her. She was wearing a flowing orange, black, and yellow caftan. She had definitely *not* been wearing that before, Katie felt sure. But how had she changed?

"Now, come on, Katie," said Norma. "Just climb down the hole after us. There really isn't any time for argument." Without hesitation, she lowered herself down the hole. "There are stairs here. You don't have to worry," she called up to Katie as she disappeared down into the blackness.

Edwina followed her down next. "Don't be afraid, sweetie," she said while her shoulders and head were still above ground. "It'll be fine."

Ned held the lantern high. "After you," he said, bowing gallantly to Katie.

"Nuh-uh," said Katie, shaking her head. "No way."

Maybe they really *were* spies, and this was some weird kind of secret headquarters. Whatever it was, it was too dark and creepy.

Ned sighed deeply. "There's really not time to argue. I'll have to go on without you if you don't want to come." He lowered himself into the hole. By the lantern light, Katie could see the wooden ladder he was climbing down. She folded her arms and turned away. She wasn't getting into any hole in the ground with these three.

As Ned's light became nothing but a dim glow shining up from the hole, Katie felt the blackness of the woods enfold her like a blanket. She held up her hand and could barely see it.

A horrible animal shrieking came from the woods, not far off. It sounded as if some animal was being attacked. What was attacking it? An owl? A wolf? A bear?

"Wait up," she called, dropping to a sitting position at the edge of the hole.

Gooseflesh formed on Katie's arms as the animal kept shrieking. Being in a hole with three strange characters and a light suddenly seemed better than being in the pitch black by herself.

Ned's lantern lit her way as she climbed down the ladder. "This way," Norma said, beckoning them to follow her.

Katie followed the others into a tunnel supported by wooden beams. "This is an old escape route," Ned explained. "It should lead us to your friends."

"How do you know?" Katie asked skeptically.

"Good guess," Ned replied cryptically.

"I sure hope you're right," Katie told him.

They traveled through the narrow, stuffy tunnel for nearly ten minutes. At one point, the walls got so narrow they had to squeeze through. The ceiling of the tunnel grew lower and lower until Katie and the others had to crouch over. Just when Katie felt she couldn't stand to be in the cramped, almost airless space anymore, Norma and Edwina stopped ahead of her.

A crude wooden door blocked their way. "Now what?" Katie groaned.

Norma placed both hands on the door. For a moment, Katie thought she saw a glow come from beneath Norma's palms. But in a blink, it was gone. *Probably just a reflection from the lantern*, Katie decided logically.

The next moment the door swung open easily.

"Thank goodness!" cried a familiar voice.

"Ashley!" Katie cried out joyfully as she squeezed past Edwina and Norma.

Ashley sat huddled against the wall of the shaft. Christina was asleep beside her, her face ashen. Ashley's teeth chattered with cold. "She just fell asleep a little while ago," Ashley said, nodding toward Christina.

"How are you?" Katie asked Ashley.

"My head aches, and I'm freezing."

"But it's not cold," said Katie.

"You're nuts," Ashley laughed weakly. She looked up at the opening in the shaft. "Warm air is coming from the tunnel there, though. Maybe you're right. I'm not cold anymore, either. I'm so glad you found help." She looked up at Edwina, Norma, and Ned. "Thank you so much for coming."

"Our pleasure," said Norma. She helped Ashley to her feet while Edwina bent over Christina and gently shook her awake.

Christina's eyes fluttered open. "I knew you'd come," she mumbled groggily.

Ned carefully helped Christina to her feet. She leaned heavily on him. "This girl's arm needs attention," he said. "Let's go."

Holding his lantern high, he led the others back through the tunnel. Clumps of dirt fell on Katie as she went. At one point, when Katie stopped to wipe her forehead, she realized she was panting. It was hard to breathe in the dark tunnel. "Keep moving," Ned called over his shoulder.

When they got to the open space where they'd climbed down, Katie was amazed at Ned's strength as he effortlessly lifted Christina up the ladder in his arms.

"Is this the way out?" Ashley asked Katie.

"Yeah," Katie said.

"Lucky thing you found it," said Ashley as she began to climb up the ladder.

"Mmmm, lucky," Katie agreed thoughtfully. Unbelievably lucky. What was really going on here?

"It really did get warm," Ashley said to Katie when they reached the woods once again. "I'm not cold at all."

"I know. Isn't it strange?" Katie agreed.

She and Ashley followed Ned, Norma, and Edwina as they helped Christina through the woods. Christina was nearly faint with the pain in her arm. She staggered along as though she were in a trance.

"How does your head feel?" Katie asked Ashley. "You were out cold."

"It hurts. Christina said I woke up pretty quickly, though," said Ashley. "Who are these people? Where did you find them?"

"Their names are Ned, Norma, and Edwina. They were on a bridge. It was the Angels Crossing Bridge!"

"You found it?" Ashley gasped.

"More like *it* found *me*. I fell, and I must have been knocked out, too. When I woke up, there I was. And there *they* were. They helped me, and then they came to find you." Katie put her hand on Ashley's arm. "They knew my name, Ashley. And they knew Christina was chanting."

A puzzled expression swept Ashley's face. "That's impossible. Are you sure?"

"I know it's impossible, but they knew."

"They look like hippies," Ashley commented quizzically. "You know, like people from the 1960s. Alice, Christina's mother, has pictures of herself and her friends wearing clothing like theirs."

Katie took a hard look at Ned, Edwina, and Norma. Ashley was right. They looked exactly like hippies. Katie was sure their clothes had changed, but she just couldn't remember how.

Ned sensed Katie's stare and returned her gaze with a smile. "Do I look okay?" he asked, bemused. "How are we doing?"

"Um, okay, I guess," Katie said, not knowing what to think. Hadn't they had this conversation before? "You, uh, you look like a bunch of hippies," she blurted. "You know, from the sixties, or whatever."

"Darn!" said Ned. "I was sure we'd gotten it right this time."

"But, Ned, how did you—" Katie began.

"Oh, well, there's no time to worry about it now," Ned cut in before Katie could finish. "We'd better keep moving."

"What's going on, Katie?" Ashley asked. "Did they change or something?"

"I don't know," Katie mumbled. "Maybe I just thought they did. I'm not sure now. Come on."

In another ten minutes, Katie could see lights ahead among the trees. It looked like people wandering around with flashlights. She and Ashley broke away and ran toward the lights. "Help!" Katie called out. "We need help!"

The people started running toward them. "Ashley! Christina!" a woman called.

"They're here!" Katie shouted back.

A woman with short blonde hair dressed in a heavy jacket and jeans was the first person Katie could see clearly. "I'm Christina's mother," the woman said frantically. "Is she with you?"

"Yes," said Katie, "but her arm's broken, I think." Christina's mother swung her flashlight through the trees until the light encircled Christina, who was slumped against a tree.

"Christina! Christina!" she cried, running toward her.

Katie looked for Ashley and found her standing among a woman, a man, and two teenaged boys. Ashley hugged the woman, who smiled happily. Katie could tell she must be Ashley's mother. The two boys and the man had the same curly red hair as Ashley. They had to be her father and older brothers.

A pang of jealousy hit Katie hard. No one was even looking for her.

It hurt.

She looked around for Edwina, Norma, and Ned. She should at least thank them. Weird as they were, they'd surely saved her and her friends' lives.

But she didn't see them. "Ned," she called. "Edwina! Norma!"

There was no answer.

Ashley joined Katie. "Where did they go?"

"I don't know." She walked back several steps into the woods. "Ned? Edwina? Norma?"

"It's as if they disappeared," said Ashley, coming alongside her.

Katie nodded. "This is so strange."

"It sure is," Ashley agreed. "Where could they have gone to?"

"They said they were angels—maybe they flew away," Katie joked.

"Angels?" Ashley asked sharply.

"That's what they said," Katie told her. "I have no idea who they really were. Angels, ha! Can you believe it?"

Ashley didn't smile. "What if they were?"

"Get real," said Katie.

"I know it's unbelievable, but . . ." Ashley's words were cut off as a large dog ran up to her and licked her hand. It was the same dog Katie had last seen sleeping on Ashley's porch.

"Wow! They even got you out to look for me, didn't they, Champ?" Ashley said, petting the dog's golden coat. "I left my parents a note, but it fell off the refrigerator magnet. It's after nine. They only found the note fifteen minutes ago. They've been worried to death."

Katie wondered if anyone at all was worried about her. Suddenly she shivered, and her teeth began to chatter. The temperature had dropped drastically. It was freezing now.

"Wow, it's getting cold again," said Ashley, hugging herself. "This weather is bizarre. We'd better call your aunt and uncle and let them know you're all right."

"They don't care," said Katie. "Do you see them out here looking for me?"

"How could they?" replied Ashley. "They have no idea you're here."

Katie's mouth went dry. Ashley was right. She'd forgotten to call them. "Uh-oh," she said. "I think I'm in big trouble."

Ashley's mother joined them. "Mom, this is Katie," Ashley introduced.

"Hello. Are you all right, dear?" Mrs. Kingsley asked.

"Yeah, I think so," Katie replied.

"Mom, Katie saved us," Ashley told her mother. "She went looking for help and found those people I told you about."

"How odd that they just left like that," murmured Mrs. Kingsley, peering into the woods. She turned back to Katie. "You're a real heroine, Katie. Thank you very much."

"You're welcome," Katie said, touched by Mrs. Kingsley's gratitude. "But I didn't really do anything."

"Someone less brave might have panicked or fallen apart completely. You were very courageous." Mrs. Kingsley hugged Ashley's shoulders. "Believe me, I appreciate it."

Mr. Kingsley, a tall man with a weathered face and deep blue eyes, came over. Ashley introduced Katie and told him what had happened. "Thank goodness you were there, Katie," he said sincerely. "I wish those other folks had stuck around. I'd like to thank them, as well."

"Katie," Mrs. Kingsley said. "Your parents must be worried to death."

The mention of her parents hurt. "I live with my aunt and uncle," she muttered. "I don't think they're worried."

"Of course they are," said Mrs. Kingsley. "Come on. I'll drive you home."

Home, Katie thought bitterly. How could Mrs. Kingsley drive her home? She didn't have one.

12

Dear Journal,

You won't believe how much trouble I'm in! I'm totally grounded for, like—forever! And all because I didn't call and say where I was going after school, which wasn't even my fault.

Man, was Uncle Jeff furious! You should have seen him when I got there (which was pretty late, I must admit.) The Kingsleys might think I'm a heroine, but *he* didn't. His face was completely red, and the veins on his neck were popping out. It was awful.

Aunt Rainie just kept shaking her head, like she was *deeply* disappointed in me. They didn't even want to hear my explanation. I tried to explain, but Uncle Jeff kept saying, "There is no excuse for this kind of thoughtless behavior." They just sent me to my room without anything to eat (which is no big loss in that house, when you think about Aunt Rainie's cooking).

I tried to call and tell them where I was going. I tried all day! But the line was always busy. Aunt Rainie gets on that phone and it's gab, gab, gab, all afternoon. She's like a human talking machine! Of course, Uncle Jeff is way too cheap to get Call Waiting like we used to have at home.

I meant to call again, but it just slipped my mind. And then I wasn't able to call at all.

Here's why I couldn't call at all. To make a long story short: I went into the woods with some friends, and they fell into an old mining shaft. When I went for help, I fell down a hill and hit my head, too. I conked out, and I must have been lying there for awhile.

But then I was saved by these three strange people.

Well, I *thought* they were incredibly strange at the time, but now I'm wondering if I was just dreaming some of the strange things about them.

This is my idea about what really happened. When I woke up from hitting my head, I might have seen the three of them and then fallen back to sleep and had a dream about them.

I dreamed they told me they were angels, and that they were dressed in old-fashioned clothing. In my dream, they thought it was 1933! I even dreamed they knew my name, and that the one named Norma knew that

Christina (one of the girls I was with) was chanting. (Yes, chanting. Christina's on the wacky side. I'll tell you about her some other time.)

I think I must have been sleepwalking through the woods with them before I really came fully awake. (Hitting my head probably made me extra-groggy.) That's why when I truly woke up, I was already standing and walking.

I bet it's also why their clothing seemed to change mysteriously. The first set of clothing they wore must have been in my dreams, and the second set was what they were really wearing.

It's all still kind of jumbled up in my head, and I'm trying to sort it out. But I have an idea about who those three were.

How does this sound? Their parents were hippies who went out into the woods to live on the land a long time ago. That would explain their hippie-style clothing and why they knew the woods so well. They all had the same strange-colored eyes, and said they were brother and sisters. (I know that part was real, not a dream.) So, I figure, maybe their parents took drugs or something and it gave them those spooky eyes.

It's the best explanation I can think of. And it would explain why they ran away like they did when they saw Ashley's family looking for us. They don't want anyone to know that they're somebody might make them leave the woods, and living in the woods is the only life they've ever known—so, naturally, they don't want anyone to know they're there.

I made the mistake of telling Ashley that they said they were angels (which was just part of my dream, but at first I thought they'd really said it). Ashley told Christina, and now the two of them think we really *saw* angels.

Christina says they saved our lives!

Of course, that's a crazy idea. I'm sure we would have gotten out of the woods sooner or later, anyway. Ashley's parents were already searching, and they would have found us eventually.

Still, I'm glad we didn't have to spend a long, cold night in the woods before we were found. The three strangers really were pretty nice. I've never met people quite like them before.

Meeting them gave me an idea for a story I'd like to write. I could make up a beginning and tell about their parents going into the woods. (I'll have to go the library and read about hippies.) I like writing, and I've always wanted to write a short story. I think this might make a pretty good first story.

I wonder if I could sell my story to a magazine or somewhere like that. And then I could make some money and get out of here.

Speaking of writing, Addy sent me another of her crummy postcards. Aunt Rainie handed it to me right before I was banished to my room. The picture of Pearl Jam on the front of the postcard was cool. But these postcards are getting on my nerves. I write her these long letters, and all I get back are postcards that don't say much of anything. It's pretty disappointing. I thought Addy was my best friend, but I guess she's forgotten about me already—or she'd like to forget about me. Maybe I should give up on her and stop writing her letters. But if I did that, I wouldn't have any friends at all anymore. (Ashley is cool, but you can't call someone a friend after one time together.)

After I write about the three strangers, I could write another story about myself and call it "The Girl Who Had No Friends."

That thought made Katie feel sad. She didn't like thinking of herself as someone with no friends, even if it was true. Katie shut her journal, then flopped back in bed and yawned. She was tired, and her head ached where she'd hit it.

She felt too keyed up to sleep, though. Her mind was racing. She couldn't stop thinking about Ned, Edwina, and Norma.

Katie had their faces in her mind as she drifted off to sleep. She dreamed she was five years old and riding her new two-wheeler. The bike was out of control and careening out toward the street. Then she was crashing into someone. She heard the squeal of brakes and shouting. She felt herself hit the cement.

In her dream, Katie looked up and saw Norma standing over her. Her violet blue eyes were warm and caring. She was dressed in white, and she had gorgeous, soft feathery wings. A golden light came from somewhere behind her head.

Katie's eyes snapped open, and she sat upright in bed, rubbing her eyes.

What a dream!

As she came awake, she gazed at the fat cherubs on her silvery wallpaper. That's what angels were. Cute little creatures someone thought up long ago—about as real as the tooth fairy.

Katie went to her backpack, which she'd tossed in the corner of the room, and fished out her cigarettes. "It's time I really smoked one of these things," she muttered to herself. She took a cigarette from the pack and put it to her lips. But where was her lighter? She searched for it in her jacket, which she'd slung onto the hook behind the door. It wasn't there. *Must have dropped it when I slipped down the hill,* she thought.

Tossing the cigarette pack on her dresser, Katie went back to bed. But she didn't want to have any more strange dreams. She wasn't even tired anymore.

She fished a pen and her spiral notebook from English class from her backpack. This was as good a time as any to start writing her story.

Edwina, Ned, and Norma were born in the woods. It was the only life they'd ever known. Their mother and father had been part of a

group of hippies who wanted to live a natural
life.

Katie thought a minute, tapping her pen against her
notebook.

As they grew up, they got the idea that they
weren't people, that they were angels. Of
course, this was a crazy idea. But that's what
they thought.

13

The next day in school, Katie was glad to see Ashley. "How are you feeling?" she asked.

"All right," Ashley replied as they walked toward homeroom together. "My parents were worried, since I'd been unconscious for a few minutes. They took me to the hospital for a checkup, but I'm okay. I just have some scratches. I don't have a concussion or anything."

"Good," said Katie. "How's Christina?"

"She's got a cast." Ashley wrinkled her nose. "Her arm is broken in *two* places. She's not in school today." Ashley stopped in the hall and looked at Katie seriously. "I couldn't stop thinking about those people who saved us. I know you don't believe it, but, Katie, the more I think about them, the more I keep thinking that they really *were* angels."

"Oh, come on," Katie scoffed.

"Seriously. My mother told me that she didn't see anyone at all. She didn't even see the light from Ned's lantern. Where did they come from? You told me they knew Christina was chanting. How could they have known that? How did they know your name?"

"I think I dreamed some of that stuff while I was trying to come awake," Katie told her. "I'm not sure anymore what was real and what wasn't."

"What *is* real is that three strangely dressed people with unusual eyes appeared out of nowhere, knew exactly how to save us, and then vanished," Ashley insisted. "And no one else saw them but us."

Just then, the bell for homeroom rang.

"And what about the weather?" Ashley added as they went into the classroom. "My mother told me it never got warm last night. It just kept getting colder and colder. Why were we so warm when we were with them?"

"I don't know," Katie said, throwing out her arms in exasperation. "But I don't believe in angels."

As they entered the classroom, they passed Darrin. "Hey, new kid," he called in a taunting tone. "That's some black and blue on your forehead. I guess you finally mouthed off to the wrong person, huh?"

"Shut up, Darrin," Katie and Ashley said together in one voice.

They left Darrin frowning deeply after them. "I'm so sorry. I didn't even ask how you were," Ashley apologized. "Did you go to the doctor to check your head yet?"

"My aunt and uncle were too busy yelling about how irresponsible I am even to ask what happened to me."

"Really?" Ashley cried, aghast.

"Well, Aunt Rainie asked if I was all right," Katie

admitted, "but when I said, 'yeah,' she just dropped it."

"How *do* you feel?" Ashley asked.

"I feel fine, I guess. But I did hit my head, and it still aches a little. I *was* unconscious, after all."

"Do you have a headache or feel sick to your stomach?" Ashley asked. Katie shook her head. "Then you probably don't have a concussion."

"But your parents took you to the hospital to make sure you were all right. My *parents* would have taken me, too. My real parents." At the mention of her parents, Katie's face seemed to crumple inwards.

Ashley laid a sympathetic hand on her shoulder. Katie hadn't told her or anyone about her parents, and she didn't want to talk about them now. For one thing, at that moment she was afraid she might cry if she talked about them. And she didn't want to cry.

"I'm all right," Katie said gruffly as she shrugged Ashley's hand off. "My aunt and uncle are just jerks, that's all."

Mr. Palmero walked in, and Katie took her seat. She was grateful for the interruption. She didn't want to talk about or even think about her aunt and uncle any more than she absolutely had to.

For the rest of the morning, until lunch, Katie had a hard time paying attention in class. The events in the woods completely occupied her mind. She *had* dreamed that Edwina, Ned, and Norma said they were angels— and that they knew her name and changed their clothes and made the temperature warmer and knew about Christina, and all. Hadn't she? Of course she had.

Still, what if she hadn't? What if she had met real

angels. They *were* on the Angels Crossing Bridge, weren't they? And so much about them had been odd. . . .

How wonderful to think they might have been angels. Real angels!

No! They weren't angels, and there was no use thinking they might have been—not even for a moment. If angels were watching out for her, her parents wouldn't have gone off for the weekend and never returned. She wouldn't be stuck here now in Pine Ridge without anyone who cared what happened to her.

In the lunchroom, Katie unwrapped the baloney sandwich she'd made the night before. "Hi," Ashley said as she pulled out the chair beside her. Katie smiled. This would be the first time since she came to Pine Ridge that she wouldn't be eating lunch alone.

"I called Christina from the pay phone," said Ashley. "She wants us to come and see her after school today."

"I can't. I'm grounded."

"That is so unfair!" said Ashley. "You tried to call. And you helped save us. You're a heroine. My parents think so. So does Christina's mom."

"That's not how Aunt Rainie and Uncle Jeff see it."

Ashley plunked her chin on her hands thoughtfully. "If you were asked to stay after school and help a teacher, would they let you?"

"I don't know. I could ask."

"Ask," Ashley urged her. "Christina says she really needs us to come over. She said it's really, truly important."

"What do you think it's about?"

"I'm not sure. But last night the doctor told her

mother—who told my parents, who told me—that Christina might experience some nightmares and even waking terrors, since she'd been through a traumatic experience. Breaking her arm made it even worse for her than it was for us. He said the most helpful thing would be for her to talk about the experience, especially with us, since we went through it with her."

"Do you think she needs to talk about things with us?" Katie asked.

"That must be what it is," Ashley agreed. "If you really can't come, I guess you could call her."

"Are you kidding? Do you think I could pry the phone out of Aunt Rainie's hands?"

"Then come home with me today. I can get my brother Jason to drive you home."

Katie pushed her chair back and got up. "I'll try to call now and see what Aunt Rainie says." She hurried out to the lobby and used the pay phone. To her amazement, she didn't get a busy signal. Then as the phone rang and rang, Katie remembered it was one of the days Aunt Rainie worked in the beauty parlor.

She didn't know the phone number of the beauty parlor, and she couldn't even remember its name. But if Aunt Rainie was working, it meant she wouldn't get home until six o'clock. Uncle Jeff always hung around work longer on the days Aunt Rainie worked so that he could pick her up and drive her home. They'd both be gone until six, and if the weather was good, Mel was usually out riding his motorcycle with his friends or hanging out at the Pine Ridge Garage.

Katie hurried back to Ashley in the lunchroom. No

need to bother Ashley with the details. "I can come, but I *have* to be back by five-thirty."

"No problem," Ashley assured her with a smile.

That afternoon, Katie once again took the bus home with Ashley. They walked down the road to the cabin where Christina and her mother lived. When they knocked on the door, Christina answered. Her arm was in a cast from above her elbow all the way to her hand. She smiled when she saw them. "I'm so glad you came," she said.

"How are you feeling?" asked Ashley as she entered a cozy room decorated in shades of brown, slate blue, and earthy red. A wind chime over the door tinkled gently as they entered. A fire crackled in the small stone fireplace. Above it hung a picture of timber wolves gazing out through some pine branches.

"I don't feel too bad," Christina replied. She looked much better than Katie had expected, and she seemed to have energy.

"Do you want to talk about what happened?" Katie offered, remembering what Ashley had told her at lunchtime.

"Yes, I do," said Christina eagerly, her blue eyes lit with excitement. She sat on the brown velvet couch and leaned forward excitedly. "Katie, last night Ashley told me what you said about Ned, Edwina, and Norma. About their being angels. Something very amazing has happened to us. We have had an actual encounter of the angelic kind!"

"Give me a break!" cried Katie. "Is that what was so important?"

"What could be *more* important?" Christina countered.

"They were *not* angels!" said Katie, shaking her head. "Their names were Ned, Edwina, and Norma Galen. Ned told me so himself. Did you ever hear of angels with last names?"

"Oh, my gosh," Ashley exclaimed. "Did you say *Galen*?"

"Yeah?" Katie answered. "Why?"

"*Galen*. Think about the letters in that name. It's an anagram," said Ashley.

"What's that?" Katie questioned her.

"That's when the letters in a word spell another word, only they're all scrambled up," Ashley explained. "The letters in *Galen* spell—"

"*Angel*," Christina supplied in a whisper.

Katie looked to Ashley and then to Christina. "Get off it, you two. I think they're just three strange characters who live out there in the woods. You know, we were all pretty shook up, so they seemed like angels to us. You always hear about how your mind plays tricks on you sometimes when you're in a tough spot. Why, just the other day I actually thought I felt the spirits of my . . ." Katie let her voice trail off. She didn't feel like talking about what she'd thought the other day.

"The spirits of who?" Christina pressed gently.

Katie looked down. "My parents. They died in a car crash. That's why I came here to Pine Ridge, to live with my aunt and uncle," she mumbled.

"Oh, I'm so sorry," said Christina.

No one said anything for a few moments. Katie got to her feet. "I'd better get home. I'm supposed to be grounded and all."

"Wait," said Christina. "I wanted you both to come here today so that we could go back into the woods and try to find the angels. I think it's important that we at least try to thank them."

"No way," said Katie, heading for the door.

"The spirits may still be nearby. This might be our only chance to contact them again before they move on," Christina insisted.

"Sorry, but not me," said Katie.

"I'll take a kitten," Christina said quickly.

"What?" asked Katie.

"Ashley said you were trying to find homes for some kittens. I'll take one."

"Great!" said Katie.

"*If* you come into the woods with us. Please. It won't take long. The three of us should be there, since we were there last night."

"I think you not only broke your arm, but you got cracked in the head, too," Katie told her.

"You'd only have one more kitten to worry about if Christina takes one," Ashley coaxed her.

"You guys are trying to bribe me!" Katie cried.

"So?" Ashley replied.

Katie glared at Christina. "Bribery is *not* exactly a spiritual thing to do."

Christina shrugged innocently. "It's for a good cause," she said.

It would be good if she could find a home for another kitten, Katie thought with a defeated sigh. "All right, but let's do whatever this is now. I have to get home."

"Thanks," Christina said, getting off the couch. She picked up her long purple cape, and Ashley helped her get it on over her cast. "Come on," she said, heading out the door. "Oh, wait. I have to leave Mom a note. She's taking a group out for a trail ride."

"Isn't it cold?" Ashley questioned.

Christina shrugged. "They wanted to go. Would you write the note, Ashley? I can't write well with my left hand."

Ashley wrote the note, and they left the house. Together, they crossed over toward the stable. "Want to see the cutest horse?" Ashley asked Katie as they walked by the stable.

"Sure," Katie agreed.

"Oh, I know. You mean Junior," said Christina. "He *is* cute."

Ashley pushed open the stable door. Katie and Christina followed her into the stable. Many of the stalls closest to the door were empty. Katie guessed the horses were out on the ride. But in one of the stalls stood a small palomino. "This is Junior," said Ashley as the three of them stepped into the stall with him. "He's nine months old. Most horses leave their mothers by nine months, but we can't get him away from May, his mother. He looks exactly like her. They're so cute together."

Katie looked around. "Where is she now?"

"Must be out on the ride," Ashley guessed.

Junior hung his head and snorted softly. Ashley patted the side of his neck. "It's all right, Junior. She'll be back soon."

"Let's get going," said Christina anxiously.

"Okay," Ashley agreed. She left the stall first. Katie was the last one out. She took a last look over her shoulder at Junior. The horse looked so sad without his mother. She knew how he felt.

"It stinks, doesn't it," she sympathized with him, lingering a moment in the stable doorway. "I know just how you feel," she muttered.

"Come on," Christina called to her.

Katie hurried to catch up with Christina and Ashley as they went around behind the stable. Together, they entered the pine woods. They'd only walked a few yards in when Christina stopped. "It took me almost two hours to prepare this spot," she said proudly.

Katie looked at the spot Christina was pointing to, then back at Christina. "Oh, come on! You really *are* nuts," she said.

14

Near a thick, ancient-looking Scotch pine, Christina had made a circle of large stones. Artificial flowers had been scattered on the stones. In the center of the circle stood a tall statue of a winged angel carved in wood. Near the statue was a glittering cluster of lavender crystals.

"What *is* all this?" asked Katie.

"A sacred circle," Christina explained excitedly, "for calling the angels back."

"Wait a minute. You were so sick you couldn't even come to school today. How on earth did you do all this?" Katie demanded.

"The doctor told my mother to keep me home today, but I didn't really feel so bad. I told her I could go in, but she insisted I stay home," Christina explained. "Besides, while I was doing this, I had the most unbelievable energy."

"You *must* have had a huge spurt of energy to move all these stones with just one hand," Katie noted.

"I know. I know. I think it must have been divine

energy. Like . . . like . . . I was *meant* to do this," said Christina, her pale skin glowing with enthusiasm.

"Where did you get all this neat stuff?" Ashley asked.

"My mother had the angel statue," said Christina, moving a crystal closer to it. "She believes in angels. The crystals are for heightening and focusing our energies. They're sort of like radio antennae for energy."

"Cool," said Ashley.

Katie looked sharply at Ashley with raised eyebrows. Cool? Was she actually into this, too?

"Assuming for a minute that those three were really angels—and I'm not saying they were —- but *if* they were, why do we want them back?" Katie questioned.

Christina looked at Katie with disbelief. "Why would we *not* want them back?" She put her hand on Katie's shoulder and spoke passionately. "Katie, we have been visited by angels. *Angels!* That doesn't happen everyday. To be touched by the presence of angels—think of it! This could change our entire lives."

"Like how?" Katie asked impatiently.

"Well, I don't know, but it's got to. Don't you see it? This will bring us closer to the spiritual side of life," said Christina.

"It couldn't hurt, could it?" Ashley offered diplomatically.

"Do you really believe in this?" Katie challenged her.

"Well, I honestly don't know. But I think it's *possible* that they were angels. I read the other day that the president's wife believes in angels, and she's a very intelligent person. Millions of people believe in angels. I read a magazine article about it not long ago. Angels have been around for centuries. The article said

Christians, Jews, and Muslims all have stories in their religions about the appearance of angels. It's definitely possible," Ashley replied decidedly.

Katie sighed and shook her head. "All right. Let's just do this stupid thing and get it over with. I have to get home."

"First, we should stand in the circle and hold hands," said Christina.

Katie rolled her eyes, but she got into the circle and took Ashley's hand. Christina stood on the left side of Ashley and clasped her hand. She closed her eyes and threw back her head. "Oh, angels of the piny woods," she intoned grandly. "We thank you for saving our lives. We feel blessed by your presence. Now we will do a dance in your honor."

"Oh, no way!" cried Katie, dropping Ashley's hand.

"Come on, just do it," Ashley insisted.

Sighing even more loudly, Katie followed Christina and Ashley as they twirled and skipped in a circle. Her own movements were halfhearted. *I would just die if anyone saw me*, she thought miserably.

When they finished dancing, Christina sat down on a rock, nodding for Ashley and Katie to sit, as well. "Now we will invoke the harmonics of the universe to call you to us."

"The what of the what?" asked Katie.

"We're going to chant the *om* sound," Christina explained. "It's a way of becoming one with the universe, which should draw the angels closer to us."

"How do *you* know?" asked Katie quarrelsomely.

"I *don't* know, but I'm doing the best I can," Christina shot back angrily. She took a deep breath and calmed herself. "Now, come on, we can't have disharmony in our circle or everything will be ruined."

Christina shut her eyes and began to make a long, vibrating sound. "Oooooo-mmmmmmmmm."

Ashley followed her. "Oooooo-mmmmmmmm."

Katie tried it. "Uh-ummmm."

Christina opened one eye. "No, not *um, ooooo-mmmmmm.*"

"OOOOO-mmmmm," Katie corrected herself.

The chanting continued. *This is ridiculous*, thought Katie. There was as much chance of angels appearing as there had been of her seeing the spirits of her parents the other day in the woods. *I'm out of here*, Katie said to herself as she silently got to her feet. Quietly, she slipped away from the stone circle as Christina and Ashley continued to chant.

She walked back through the woods until she came out behind the stables. Rounding the corner of the stable, she spotted something moving off to her right. It was Junior, the young palomino. "Oh, no!" Katie cried softly. "He got out of the stable." She wondered if it had been her fault. Had she closed his stall correctly? Had she left the stable door open?

Katie ran to the horse. When he saw her, he backed away fearfully and whinnied. "Come on, Junior," she tried to coax him gently. "Come back to the stable."

The horse kept backing up. *This isn't going to work*, Katie told herself. Then she remembered what Ashley had said about Junior wanting to be near his mother, May. If she could find May, maybe she could lure Junior back before he ran off into the woods.

Katie hurried back to the stable and looked inside. Most of the horses were still out. But just then, she heard some noise outside the stable. Running back outside, she saw that the riders were returning from their trail ride. Katie spotted a palomino horse that just had to be May. She hurried over to the heavy-set woman dismounting May. "Can I borrow that horse a minute?" Katie requested urgently.

"I suppose so," said the woman.

May snorted and stamped her feet when Katie took hold of the reins. Katie tried to be more gentle—maybe she was handling May too roughly. She looked around for Christina's mother but didn't see her anywhere. Checking back, she saw Junior on the edge of the woods.

"Come on, Junior, your mom is here," Katie called to the horse. Anxious to show Junior that his mother was back, Katie pulled on May's reins. May stamped again and jerked her head back, yanking the reins from Katie's hands.

With a high whinny, May ran in a circle. She spotted Junior and ran toward him. Her excitement set off the other horses. They pulled away from the riders who were in the process of dismounting. Two women were thrown to the ground as six other horses pulled away and began running with May.

"Oh, no!" Katie cried, running after May. "No! Come back! Whoa, horses! Whoa! Stop!" Her heart pounded. How could this be happening!

The horses hooves sounded like thunder as they raced around her. *They're going to trample me!* she thought, terrified. But the horses rapidly passed her by.

"No!" Katie cried. May and Junior were dashing into the woods. The other horses were following.

Christina's mother came racing out of the stable. "What happened?" she shouted.

"I didn't mean to," Katie sobbed. "I was just trying to bring May to Junior."

Ashley's mother and father ran from the main house. "What's going on, Alice?" Mr. Kingsley asked Christina's mother.

"The horses broke free for some reason," Alice reported anxiously. "Katie said something about Junior and May."

"Well, I was trying to help Junior . . ." Katie stammered. Alice looked unhappy, but the Kingsleys looked annoyed. They weren't listening, anyway. They were all already charging toward the stable.

Jeremy and Jason ran out of the house. "Saddle up quick, fellas," Mr. Kingsley told his sons. "We've got to round up those horses fast before they get too far."

Ashley and Christina came running out from behind the barn. "What's going on?" cried Ashley. "We just saw the horses go racing past us through the woods."

"It seems Katie started a stampede," Mr. Kingsley said bitterly as he hurried into the stable.

"Katie!" Ashley gasped in dismay. "What did you do?"

Katie wished desperately that she could just disappear. "I didn't mean to. I was only trying to—"

She cut herself off as a familiar beat-up Jeep rumbled up the dirt road. Katie's pounding heart crashed into her stomach. It was Aunt Rainie and Uncle Jeff!

15

Silently, Katie walked into her aunt and uncle's kitchen, feeling like a prisoner walking down death row. Uncle Jeff slammed the kitchen door behind him. His face was red, and the veins on his neck popped out like cords of rope. His blue eyes blazed.

"We're going to have to pay for that one horse they couldn't retrieve. You know that don't you?" He spoke between clenched teeth.

Katie nodded, too frightened to speak. Uncle Jeff had spent the last two hours helping to round up the horses. All but one had been caught.

"I'm sorry," Katie said in a choked voice.

"Do you know how much a horse costs?" Uncle Jeff exploded.

Katie shook her head.

"Hundreds and hundreds of dollars!" he shouted, pounding the kitchen table violently.

"Now, Jeff," said Aunt Rainie softly.

"Don't tell me 'now Jeff'!" Uncle Jeff yelled at Aunt

Rainie. "This is the second time in two days this girl has gone off without calling. This time she deliberately defied us, knowing full well she was grounded. And when we track her down, we discover that she's recklessly set off a horse stampede."

"It wasn't a stampede," said Katie weakly.

"Don't contradict me!" Uncle Jeff yelled.

"I'm just trying to say . . . well . . . what happened with the horses . . . I didn't mean to . . . it was sort of . . ." Katie stammered in a timid, quivering voice. "I was just trying to get back—"

Aunt Rainie fretfully cut her off. "I didn't know what to think when I called home and found you weren't here yet. We called the school looking for you, and Ms. Trencher said she knew who you were because you had been to the principal's office the other day. What happened then?"

"Oh, that wasn't my fault," Katie began.

"*Nothing* is your fault!" Uncle Jeff shouted. "It's not your fault that you have your aunt worried sick all the time! It's not your fault that we had to spend hours driving all over town looking for you, and then be embarrassed at the ranch like that!"

"Now, Jeff," said Aunt Rainie, "these things can happen, and I'm sure Katie didn't mean—"

Uncle Jeff's red face got even redder. "Rainie, don't defend her," he bellowed. "Tell me this! Isn't it her fault that we are now in debt for hundreds of dollars, money we don't have? *That's* not her fault, I suppose!"

"It's not," Katie sobbed, tears spilling from her eyes at last.

Uncle Jeff turned away from her, then suddenly turned back. "Let me tell you this," he said fiercely. "You will be coming straight home from school every day from now on, and I will find work around here for you to do until that horse is paid off. I don't care how long it takes." He searched his shirt pocket and pulled out a rumpled pack of Camels. "And while we're at it, what were these doing in your room?"

"You went through my things?" Katie gasped indignantly, snatching the pack. "How dare you!"

Her mother would never have snooped in her things. This was too much!

To Katie's surprise, Uncle Jeff didn't demand the pack back. "I was just tidying up your room this morning," Aunt Rainie said meekly.

"You were tidying up my dresser drawer?" Katie challenged, not willing to believe her aunt.

"No, I was putting socks in, and—"

"Don't you talk to your aunt in that tone!" Uncle Jeff interrupted furiously.

"Why shouldn't I? You don't care about me!" Katie shouted. "I'm just a big pain to you. Well, I don't care about the two of you, either! I hate you! I wish I had gone to strangers!" she cried passionately. "I hate it here!" Overwhelmed by her own anger, Katie whirled around and raced up the stairs to her room.

She slammed the door behind her. Pulling off her backpack and flinging it to the floor, she threw herself on her bed. She pounded the pillow furiously with tightly balled fists.

Kneeling back, she lifted the pillow over her head and

smashed it against the headboard of the bed with all her strength. She smashed it again and again! How had her life become so horrible? She wished she'd been in the car with her parents that night. Death would have been better than having this awful, lonely, angry feeling inside her.

As she landed the pillow on the headboard with yet another ferocious blow, there was a knock on the door. Without waiting for a reply, Aunt Rainie put her head into the room.

Katie dropped the pillow and smoothed back her hair. *Now she'll think I'm insane*, Katie thought, embarrassed. *But so what? Who cares what she thinks?*

"You all right, honey?" Aunt Rainie asked timidly as she entered the room.

Katie folded her arms. "I'm fine," she snapped.

Aunt Rainie looked at her with a worried expression, obviously unconvinced. "You know, Jeff has a terrible temper, he always has had. If you just give him a little time to cool down, I'm sure—"

"I *said* I was fine," Katie cut her off. She wasn't going to tiptoe around Uncle Jeff and his terrible temper. If Aunt Rainie thought she was scared of him, she could forget it! Aunt Rainie was probably only saying all this because *she* was afraid of Uncle Jeff.

"Uncle Jeff went out for a little while. Why don't you come down and have some—"

"No, thank you," Katie said harshly. She wasn't about to sit and chat with Aunt Rainie, the snoop—the squealer who'd turned her cigarette pack over to Uncle Jeff, the tyrant.

"If you don't mind, I really just want to be alone," Katie continued.

Aunt Rainie's pressed her lips together and then nodded. "All right. If that's really what you want."

Aunt Rainie left, and Katie stood a moment, staring at the door. Then she grabbed her backpack from the floor, and pulled out her journal.

> Dear Journal,
>   Everything stinks! I hate my aunt and uncle—hate! hate! hate them! Which is fine since they hate me, too.
>   But guess what? After tomorrow, I'm not going to see them ever again. After tomorrow, I'm out of here. No kidding. It's *adios* Pine Ridge for me.

Katie stopped writing. Her breathing was heavy with emotion. She reread what she'd written. She'd scrawled the words almost without thinking, hardly aware of what she was writing until the words appeared on the page. But it made perfect sense. Leaving Pine Ridge was her only answer.

She went back to writing, suddenly enthusiastic about this new plan.

> Here's my idea. I've started writing that story I told you about. I'm going to go to the city and try to sell it.

Katie bit her lip thoughtfully. She had to think

seriously about money. She wouldn't have much of it until her story sold, just enough for a one-way train ticket with a little left over for food. She certainly couldn't afford a hotel room. Well, she'd sleep in the train station until she sold her story.

She continued writing, feeling positive that things would work out.

> The rest of the money I need to live, I'll make from my story. Then I'll write more stories until I have a bunch of money saved. When I have enough, I'll find an apartment. Or maybe I'll take a trip around the country and have loads of adventures that I'll write about.

Katie shut her journal and tapped her pen thoughtfully on the cover. Writing her plan down made it seem real. She was flooded with excitement. Finally she'd be getting out of here.

Shaking her pillow out of its case, Katie looked around the room, deciding what to take. She opened her dresser and threw in some underwear, socks, a crew-neck sweater.

From her top drawer she took a photo of herself with her parents. A sob choked in her throat as she looked at their smiling faces. They'd all been so happy then. She quickly dropped the photo into the pillowcase. Then she took out a twenty-dollar bill and a ten, the last of the money she'd brought with her from home, and stuffed it into her back pocket.

What else would she need?

Nothing, really. The beginning of her story was already in the notebook in her backpack. She jammed her journal and the packed pillowcase into her backpack. Tomorrow, she'd take Ashley's school bus, only she wouldn't get off at the Pine Manor Ranch. She'd noticed that the bus stopped near the train station.

At this time tomorrow, she'd be faraway in the city: free of Aunt Rainie and Uncle Jeff—and Pine Ridge—forever!

16

"You're going *where*?" Ashley exclaimed in horror the next day in school as she and Katie talked at the lunch table.

"Shhh!" Katie hissed. "I don't want the whole world to know. To the city."

"But we found the missing horse last night," Ashley argued. "Your uncle doesn't have to pay for it. And I understand what happened. And so do my parents. You couldn't help it, you didn't know how the horses would react. You were only trying to help. Now there's no reason for you to go."

"Your dad seemed really furious," Katie told her. "Your parents probably won't ever let me come over again. I wouldn't want to, anyway. I couldn't face them."

"They calmed down," Ashley assured her. "My dad was just upset because he was worried about the horses. I told him what happened and how you were just trying to help. They understand, honest, Katie. Please don't do this. "

Katie shook her head. "Thanks, but all that doesn't even matter anymore. You should have heard the way my uncle was shouting at me last night. I couldn't believe it. No one ever spoke to me like that before. Never! And I don't havc to put up with it, either."

"Maybe he just needs time to get used to you," Ashley offered.

"Yeah, sure," Katie scoffed. "And Aunt Rainie was going through my things. She found my cigarettes, and Uncle Jeff started hassling me about that, too." Katie checked her side pocket, where she'd hurriedly shoved the pack that morning.

"Well, you shouldn't smoke," said Ashley.

"That's not the point!" Katie exclaimed heatedly. "They hate me, there's no privacy, and I have to get out of there. So I'm going."

"Going where?" Christina asked, coming up behind Katie. She put her lunch bag down on the table and fumbled with it, using her left hand.

"Katie's running away from home. Today!" Ashley whispered.

"Pine Ridge *isn't* my home," Katie insisted. "Face it. I'm an orphan. I have no home. So how can I run away from home?"

"You have family and a place to live. That's a home," said Christina calmly.

"No, it's not," Katie disagreed, pushing her hot baked ziti lunch around with her fork. She didn't feel like eating. She was too tense. Last night she'd been excited about running away. Today, she was nervous. Scared, but determined to go. What other choice did she have?

Ashley put her hand on Katie's wrist. "Katie, I'm really worried about you. I've heard terrible stories about what happens to runaways down in the city. You don't want to do this."

"Yes, I do. I'm going to sell my story about what happened to us in the woods, and then write more. I'll be fine."

Christina and Ashley exchanged concerned glances. They didn't look at all convinced.

"Really," Katie said, speaking to herself as much as them. "I'll be fine."

She forced herself to choke down a bite of the ziti. It might have to hold her over for awhile, until she could buy food again. She'd have a few dollars left after she paid for her ticket, but it would have to last until she sold her story.

Katie forced another forkful into her mouth. If she was going to be on her own, she would have to start thinking about things like this.

That afternoon, Katie got on the bus with Ashley and Christina. Her backpack was heavy, crammed as it was with the extra items she'd packed.

Ashley and Christina both crowded into the seat with her, squashing Katie up against the window. "Katie, I've been thinking. You can't go," said Christina as soon as she sat down.

"Why not?" asked Katie.

"What about the kittens?" Christina said. "Do you want to be responsible for their deaths?"

The kittens. She'd forgotten all about them! Christina was right. She didn't want them to die.

She reached into her pack and dug out her small assignment pad and a pen. She scribbled her aunt and uncle's number on it, and handed the torn-out paper to Christina. "Here's the number," Katie said. "Call my aunt and tell her you and Ashley each want a kitten. Get two for Mr. Marshall, too. Try to find a home for the other one if you can. But don't give one to Darrin, whatever you do."

"Well, all right," Christina agreed reluctantly. "But I still say you shouldn't go. Really, it's a terrible idea. I did your numbers and this is a very unfavorable day for you. Something awful will happen."

"Really?" asked Katie.

Christina hung her head. She couldn't lie. "No, I didn't really do the numbers, because I didn't know you were running away until lunchtime. But if I had, it *might* have come out badly. It *will* come out badly. I just know it."

"You don't know that," Katie grumbled.

Christina grabbed Katie's hand. "I *do* know it. I have hunches about things, and a lot of times I'm right. I feel this very strongly. This isn't going to be good for you. It's not!"

Katie pulled her hand away. "I'm going," she insisted.

"I agree with Christina," said Ashley. "I've seen her hunches work out all the time. And, besides, what's the big deal about getting into trouble? So you got into a little trouble. I'm always in trouble," Ashley added. "You don't see me running away, do you?"

"When you get in trouble, people think it's cute," Katie objected. "And, you have a family, people who care about you. You know you can count on them if things get really rough. Look at how they came running out to search for you. They love you. You have a reason to stay. What do I have? My parents are dead. I live with an aunt and uncle I don't even know. My uncle wishes I wasn't there, my cousin acts as if I'm *not* there, and my aunt just puts up with me because she has this idea about me being part of her family. Well, I'm not part of that family. I have no family!"

The bus slowed down as it came to the stop near the train station. Christina grabbed the sleeve of Katie's jacket and gripped tightly. "What about the angels?" she asked in a quiet voice.

Katie smiled joylessly as she gathered up her backpack. "They'll survive without me." How could there be angels when her life was so rotten? If angels were real, why didn't they do something for her?

"I'm going to the sacred circle today, and I'm going to ask them to help you," Christina whispered fiercely.

"Thanks, but don't bother," said Katie, getting up.

"I'm going with her," said Ashley. "You're going to need help, Katie. Lots of it!"

The door of the bus was opening. Katie had to hurry. "Listen, you guys have been great. I'll miss you. Look for my story. You'll be in it." She ran up to the front of the bus and got off. The breath caught in her throat as the bus drove away.

Katie watched the bus until it was out of sight. Once the bus disappeared, she let out her breath.

She'd done it. Her adventure was beginning.

Katie felt as if a part of her life was ending and a new part was about to begin. She felt free, unattached—almost weightless, despite the burden of her full backpack.

She walked the two blocks to the Pine Ridge station and bought a one-way ticket to the city. Handing over her twenty-dollar bill, she stuffed the four dollars and fifty cents of change into her jeans pocket.

"You're in luck," said the ticket seller. "The train will be here in about ten minutes."

Katie hurried to the platform outside the ticket booth to wait for the train. She was the only person on the platform. Gazing up, she saw that the sky was filling with thick, gray clouds. It was cold, too. Unusually cold, considering that it was already the middle of March. *Would spring ever come?* she wondered.

Jamming her hands into her pockets, she paced the platform. Finally, she heard the distant whistle of the approaching train. Her heart filled with anticipation. She jumped up and down, partly to get warm and partly out of excitement.

In just a few hours she'd arrive back in the city. Back home. Sure, it might be rough at first, for a few days. But soon she'd start to meet new people, new friends. And she'd be busy selling her story.

Once it was published, she might even be famous. She pictured herself being interviewed for magazines and being invited to dinner by people who appreciated her. Maybe, when she was a famous writer, she'd even write a story about this terrible, horrible time in her life.

The train whistle blew, sending a shiver up Katie's spine.

The train was coming—the train that would carry her out of Pine Ridge. And into a wonderful new life.

When it pulled into the station, Katie got on the

nearest car. It was nearly empty. She loved the musty, overheated smell of the train. There was something exciting about trains. They went so many places, carried so many different people.

Trains were always filled with possibility.

She tossed her backpack onto the first bank of seats, a group of four seats, two facing two. She'd have room to stretch out during the long trip.

Katie sat down in the seat nearest the window. "Last call for Pine Ridge," the conductor's voice came over the speaker system.

After a few moments the doors shut with a *whoompf.*

The train engine snorted to life, and the train lurched forward.

"Tickets, please, all tickets," a tall, bearded conductor sang out in a rich, full voice.

Katie handed him her ticket. He punched it and handed it back to her. Katie stared at the hole in her ticket. This was real. She was doing it, doing what she should have done weeks ago. Nothing could stop her now.

The train hit a steady rhythm as it moved down the tracks. Katie leaned against the window and watched the creek that ran along the tracks. Billowing clouds rolled along in the sky.

She touched the warm glass with her fingertips. The future lay ahead of her at the end of these railroad tracks. *Everything will be different now, better,* she thought as she watched Pine Ridge slip away behind her, into her past.

17

Katie loved the steady, gently rocking rhythm of the train. Outside her window ever-changing landscapes swept by, framed by the window's steel rim.

After awhile, Katie opened her pack, pulled out her spiral notebook, and reread her story about Edwina, Norma, and Ned. As she read, a small frown formed on her lips and a concerned line spread across her brow.

Bor-ing, she decided unhappily when she'd finished reading the first two pages. There needed to be more dialogue. And it just didn't sound interesting enough the way she'd written it. No one would want to read this story the way it was—and that meant no one would want to buy it, either.

She tore the pages out and crumpled them. Then she took out a pen and began again. She tapped the paper thoughtfully several times, then began to write.

> When I was a girl, I met three remarkable and unusual people.

That was better, she thought. People would take the story more seriously if they thought it was written by an adult.

But what would she have the characters say? She'd just have to make things up. This was a story, after, all, not a school report.

Katie continued writing.

> Their lonely life in the dense pine forest had driven them mad. Edwina often wandered through the woods singing: "I'm an angel! An angel!" For, you see, all three of them actually believed themselves to be angels. Poor, insane creatures that they were, they really thought this was true. "Certainly, we are angels," Ned would say. "Who else lives as we do? We must be angels." And, for a few mystifying moments, I almost thought so, too. My accidental meeting with them in the woods came at a time when I was in desperate need of—"

Katie put down her pen. *What was that annoying sound?* she wondered, looking around. It had completely broken her concentration. Did someone have a small, yapping dog on the train?

She heard the sound again and realized it came from the seat directly across the aisle from hers.

A short, thin girl with scraggly black hair sat alone, hunched over. Katie hadn't even noticed her there when she got on the train.

Katie frowned, puzzled. Where had she come from? How

had she gotten into her seat without Katie seeing her? It was as though she'd simply appeared out of nowhere.

The girl's skin was so pale it appeared almost translucent under the harsh train lights. Even from across the aisle, Katie could see delicate purple veins at her temples. Her eyes were ringed with sleeplessness. Her slim shoulders shook each time she coughed—the rumbling, hacking cough that had disturbed Katie.

"Are you all right?" Katie asked, leaning toward the aisle.

The girl looked at her with large, dark eyes and coughed. "I'm all right," she said, when her coughing fit had subsided.

Katie nodded and went back to her story. *When I was in desperate need of* . . . She hesitated. Of what? In desperate need of a friend? Of help? Of directions? Of mouth-to-mouth resuscitation? All of the above?

She crossed out half the sentence she'd already written and wrote above it: *when I was really, really desperate.*

She stopped again and thought about Norma, Edwina, and Ned. They really had shown up when she needed them most. Maybe they were strange, but she owed them a lot. *Wouldn't it be wonderful if they really were angels?* she thought.

Shaking her head, she laughed bitterly. It would be wonderful if there were a Santa Claus, too. But this was the real world.

In the real world you looked after yourself as best you could. And rotten things happened anyway. There was nothing you could do about it. In the real world you were all alone. Even if you thought you had friends (like dumb Addy, who never wrote except for stupid postcards), they forgot about you, or you had to leave them. In the real world even your parents— who you thought would always be there—could go away and never come back. In the real world you got stuck with a guy like Uncle Jeff, who only cared about money, and an aunt like Aunt Rainie, who went along with Uncle Jeff because she was too chicken to stand up to him.

> Desperate though I was, I wasn't fooled by
> their claim to be angels. Little by little I learned
> the story of their real lives, how their parents
> had come into the woods as hippies and . . .

Katie put down her pen and again frowned. The girl's coughing made it impossible to think straight.

The train stopped at Cross River Junction, but no one new got on. Katie tried hard to pay attention to her story. Once she got to the city, all her energy would have to go towards selling it. It had to be ready.

It was impossible to concentrate, though, because of the coughing.

Looking over, Katie saw that the girl's face was nearly blue with the strain. When she finally stopped hacking, she glanced over at Katie apologetically. "Sorry."

"That's okay," Katie replied, feeling too badly for the girl to be truly annoyed. "That sounds terrible. What did the doctor say about it?"

The girl shook her head. "Haven't been to one."

She hadn't been to a doctor?! "Are you kidding?" asked Katie, crossing the aisle to sit beside the girl. "Why not?"

"No money," the girl replied with another short cough.

"What about your parents . . . or whoever?"

The girl looked around carefully, checking even behind her seat. "I ran away," she whispered.

Katie nodded and smiled. "Me, too."

"Shhhh," said the girl, frowning. "The conductor might hear and call the cops. They'll take you back home, you know."

"Really?" Katie said. She hadn't thought of that. "I'm Katie, by the way."

"Lee," the girl introduced herself just as another fit of coughing seized her.

"You'd better see a doctor," said Katie as the coughing died down again. "Couldn't you find a free clinic or something?"

"Some kid told me that there's a homeless shelter in Miller's Creek where they have a nurse on duty all the time," Lee said. "She's not a doctor, but she's allowed to give out medicine."

Katie consulted a schedule posted over the seats. "You're close to Miller's Creek," Katie told her. "It's the next town. We'll be there soon."

"Good," said Lee. "The kid told me you have to go around the back, because if you come in the front way, they'll ask you all kinds of stuff. If they find out you're a runaway, they'll call the cops. But once you're inside, the nurse will see you. You can tell her your mother is asleep on one of the cots or something like that."

Katie studied the girl. Her jeans were worn, and her short-sleeved cotton shirt was too light for the season. Her gray winter jacket was too big for her and torn at the pockets.

"How long has it been since you ran away?" Katie asked.

"Ummm," Lee considered. "I think I left around the beginning of September. It was so hot then, I forgot it was ever going to get cold, so I didn't pack anything warm. It was terrible until I found this jacket in the garbage two months ago. There was even ten bucks in the pocket! Pretty lucky, huh?"

"Yeah," said Katie. She counted back the months quickly. "You didn't find that jacket until the middle of January?" she exclaimed.

"Maybe the beginning of January. I'm not exactly sure. December was pretty rough without it, let me tell you. I bet that's how I got sick."

"You've been sick since December?" Katie cried.

Lee nodded. "Not *this* sick. It started out like a little cold. Then I got the cough, and it just kept getting worse. Some kids I was staying with in an old warehouse made me leave because I was keeping everyone awake at night with my coughing." Lee laughed balefully. "Isn't that the worst, being kicked out of an abandoned warehouse by a bunch of runaways?"

"That's pretty bad," Katie sympathized.

"Anyway, that's why I'm headed for Miller's Creek, because I have no place to stay now and I hope I can see the nurse."

"When did you get on the train?" Katie asked curiously. "I didn't see you."

Lee laughed again, setting off another round of coughing. "I was hiding under the seat," she finally managed to say. "I didn't want the conductor to see me, because I don't have a ticket."

"Wow, that took nerve."

Lee waved her hand. "Don't worry. You'll learn the tricks as you go along. Everybody does."

Katie was about to explain that she'd be fine, since she was going to sell her story, but she was cut short by an announcement. "Miller's Creek, next stop! Next stop, Miller's Creek!"

"Well, that's me. See ya," said Lee as she got up.

"Good luck," said Katie, watching Lee leave the train. She was about to go back to her own seat when she spotted a rumpled paper shopping bag sitting in the corner of Lee's seat. Opening it, she saw a hat, gloves, mittens, and a pair of red rubber boots.

Snapping them up, she dashed for the door. "Hey!" she cried. Lee had already stepped out onto the platform. "You forgot your stuff!" Katie shouted, waving the bag from the train doorway. Lee was walking away. She hadn't heard her.

Katie saw that people were still getting on the train. She guessed she had a minute or two to spare. Stepping out of the train, she raced down the platform. "Lee! Lee!"

Finally the girl turned around and faced Katie with questioning eyes.

"Your stuff," Katie panted, holding out the bag to her. "You forgot it."

"Oh, my gosh," said Lee as she took the bag. "Thanks, that would have been terrible."

"No problem," said Katie breathlessly.

At that very moment, the train doors shut. Katie ran to the nearest door and pounded on it. "Open up!" she shouted desperately. "Open, please!"

The door remained shut.

She dug her fingers between the black rubber door edges where they met in the center, trying to pry the doors apart, but it was no use. Slowly at first, the train pulled out of the station. Katie banged on the nearest window. "Ask them to stop!" she shouted to the woman behind it.

The woman simply looked away.

The train picked up speed rapidly. Katie raced alongside it. "Stop! Stop!"

She ran all the way to the end of the platform. Then her shoulders slumped over miserably as she watched the back end of the train pull away.

"There will be another train," said Lee coming up behind her.

"But all my stuff was on that train," Katie moaned. "*All* of it!"

18

"Here's what you do," Lee whispered to Katie as they entered the small station house at Miller's Creek. "Do it the way I did, and sneak onto the next train."

"I can't," said Katie. "I don't have the nerve. Besides, you're small. You can fit under that seat. I couldn't."

"Do you have any money at all?" Lee asked.

"The change I stuck in my back pocket," Katie said forlornly. "Four-fifty."

"All right. Here's something else you can do. You can buy a ticket to the next stop, which only costs a few dollars. You give that to the conductor. Then you don't get off at your stop. If he says anything to you, pretend you didn't realize. Cry and act real pathetic. He'll tell you to go to the end of the train line and then go back to your stop. I've stayed on the train that way for days in really cold weather." The effort of talking started Lee coughing again.

"All right," Katie agreed. "I'll try that." By looking at the train schedule posted over the ticket sales window, she discovered that the town of Fishington was the next stop.

"How much is a ticket to Fishington?" she asked the man selling tickets.

"Three-seventy-five," he told her.

Katie pushed her money through the window and he handed her back her ticket. "When's the next train to Fishington?" she asked.

The man looked at a schedule. "Not for another three hours. Six-forty-seven."

"Six-forty-seven!"

"Most of the trains coming through here around now are express trains," the ticket seller explained apologetically. "They pass Miller's Creek and Fishington right by."

Katie went back to Lee, who had taken a seat on a bench by the door. "I have three hours to kill," she reported glumly.

"Too bad," said Lee. "Thanks for bringing me my stuff, though. It took me months to find all this stuff. It looks like I'm going to need it, too. It's getting awfully cold, and it sure looks like it's going to snow."

Katie frowned. "You think so?" she asked, gazing out the window of the ticket station. The clouds now formed a heavy gray blanket.

"It does to me," said Lee. "I've gotten pretty good at figuring out when it's going to snow or rain. It helps."

"I guess so."

Katie slumped gloomily down beside Lee. "Now what am I going to do?" she mumbled, letting her chin drop into her hands. "I had ten dollars in that pack, all my clothes, a bag of chips, and . . ." Katie's jaw dropped in dismay.

"And what?" Lee asked.

"A picture," Katie said quietly. "A picture that was really important to me—of my parents. They're dead."

"Could you get another picture?" asked Lee.

"My aunt has all the albums now. And I'm never going back there again."

"Oh," said Lee. "I'm sorry. Really sorry. It must be real tough to be an orphan."

Lee put her hand sympathetically on Katie's shoulder. Suddenly, unexpectedly, Katie was awash in tears. She covered her face with her hands.

It was as if every kind thing that anyone had said to her since her parents' car accident—all the soft murmurs, the gentle words, the soothing caresses—everything she'd blocked out and hadn't let herself respond to, was contained in Lee's simple expression of sympathy.

Katie felt like she'd been in a dream that she was suddenly awakening from.

In the last few weeks she hadn't really heard anyone, not really. She'd been too stunned, too shocked by what had happened.

She'd experienced small waves of emotion in fits and starts, as if the feelings were trying to break through, but she'd held them tightly back.

Now all the words, the feelings, the reality of it all flooded her as if a dam had broken open, had burst from the strain of too much pushing against it.

She cried hard, glad to be crying, glad to let it all

come rushing out. She was so sad about her parents dying, sadder than she'd realized. The sadness had been down in her bones, in her muscles.

And now the sadness was coming out. Her body was finally releasing some terrible thing it had been clutching inside—a thing that needed, desperately needed, to be released.

A heavier flood of tears rushed forward, drenching her cheeks. She was so glad to weep without control.

So, so deeply glad.

Lee kept her arm around Katie while she cried, holding on with a gentle pressure. "It's all right," said Lee. "Cry as much as you want."

After awhile, her tears spent themselves. Katie slumped forward, exhausted.

19

Almost as soon as Katie stopped crying, Lee began coughing again.

The man behind the ticket window leaned forward to see what was going on.

"We're some pair," said Katie to Lee. "Sobbing and coughing. What a noise we make."

Lee nodded as she tried to control her coughing. "We'd better move on," she said quietly when her coughing fit passed. "That ticket seller is still looking at us. You're crying, and I don't look so good. He may have figured out something is up with us."

"All right," Katie agreed. She didn't want to leave the warm ticket house to go out into the cold, but she figured Lee was more experienced in these things than she was.

They stepped outside and were instantly buffeted by a bitter, cold wind. "I have an idea," said Lee. "Why don't you come with me to the shelter? You'll get a free meal there, and you can stay warm until it's time for you to come back and get your train."

"Makes sense," said Katie. "Do you know where it is?"

"The kid I met told me it was up Creek Road, just a short walk from the station."

The railroad station was at the intersection of two roads that came down a hill beyond the building. They chose the nearest one, the one on the right, and were happy to find that it was named Creek Road.

Lee opened her paper bag. "Want one glove?" she offered.

"No, thanks. I'll just keep my hands in my pockets. Put that scarf and hat on, too. You need to keep warm. You're sick."

Katie pulled her cigarettes from her pocket. "At least I didn't lose *these*." Somehow she still believed in their power to make her look tough. As if she could warn people off just by sticking one in the corner of her mouth. Like a weird kind of security blanket. A more grown-up version of one, that's all. If only they could make her feel tough, too—make her *be* tough. Katie took a deep breath and reached into the pack. "Do you want one?" she asked Lee.

Lee was too busy coughing to answer.

Katie put the pack away. Offering a cigarette to a person already coughing her lungs out seemed stupid.

They headed up Creek Road until they came to a bleak, dark brick building that had clearly once been a school. Katie moved past the chain-link fence toward the front door, but Lee put a hand on her shoulder. "Back door, remember?"

"Oh, right, we're runaways. I forgot."

Katie followed Lee around toward the back of the building. They walked through an empty, desolate schoolyard until they came to a plain, gray metal door.

"The kid I met said to knock hard four times, then wait and knock again twice," said Lee. She pounded four times, then waited. After a pause, she pounded two more times.

Katie glanced at the ominous sky. She felt sure Lee was right. It would snow for certain. "We're getting in here just in time," she remarked.

Lee nodded as she coughed. When she was done, she leaned heavily against the building and held her side.

"What's wrong?" asked Katie, suddenly frightened for her.

"When I coughed that time, I got a terrible pain under my ribs, like I tore a muscle or something. Man! It hurts!" She took several slow, deep breaths then slowly straightened up. "I'll be okay," she said, still wincing in pain.

"Good thing we're going to see that nurse," said Katie.

"Give me your cigarettes," said Lee.

"I really don't think you should—"

"They're not for me," Lee cut her off. "Anything we have that we want to keep, we have to hold onto here. Lots of times, people steal your stuff in places like this. You can put anything you want in this bag."

Katie dropped her Camels and a pack of matches she'd found into the bag. Lee took off her hat, gloves, and scarf and dropped them in, too. Then she crumpled the bag as tightly as possible and stuck it inside her jacket.

Finally, a short boy with a black eye answered the door. He looked Katie and Lee over suspiciously. "Okay," he said, apparently deciding it was safe to admit them.

They walked into a room that once had been the school's locker room. Kids of all different ages lounged on the long benches and up against the faded, chipped lockers.

A chill ran through Katie as she glanced at the faces of the kids around her. Some looked scared. Others looked permanently wary and suspicious, as if they never, ever let their guards down. The kid with the black eye was one of those. Katie noticed a blonde girl who could have been a fashion model if she didn't look so very weary and sad.

And then there were other kids whose expressions were so hard and tough that they frightened Katie. She'd never seen faces like theirs before. And she thought she'd seen tough before.

As they moved past the lockers, a granite-faced girl in tight jeans and a ratty sweater put her booted foot up against a locker to block their path. "Who said you could come here?" she demanded aggressively.

"I didn't know we needed an invitation," Lee shot back with an energy that surprised Katie, considering how weak and sick Lee was.

The other girl's eyes narrowed dangerously.

"Is the nurse here?" Katie jumped in.

The girl stared at her. Katie was close to her equal in size. She hoped that would count for something. "You sick?" the girl asked.

"We just want to see the nurse," said Katie.

"The nurse ain't here until tomorrow."

"We'll just get something to eat, then," said Lee, looking down at the girl's leg, which still blocked her path. "If you'll excuse us."

"I'll *excuse* you once I get some payment," the girl said, not budging.

"We don't have anything," Lee replied.

"I bet you do," said the girl, shoving Lee back against the locker. As Lee's frail body banged into the locker, the paper bag she'd hidden in her jacket fell to the floor. Lee doubled over in a fit of coughing.

The girl bent for the bag, but Katie put her foot down on the girl's hand. "Leave our stuff alone, and leave us alone," she said, trying to match the girl's toughness.

The girl looked up at Katie with hate-filled eyes. "Nice boots," she hissed. "I think I'll take those, too."

She grabbed Katie's ankle with both hands before Katie had time to react. Katie felt herself fly backward over the bench. A sharp pain rang through her as her head hit the hard floor.

Despite the pain, Katie forced herself up onto her elbows, forced herself to open her eyes and be alert. As the room came back into focus, she saw the girl looking down at her, a switchblade in her hand.

20

"Ahhhh!" Lee shouted, jumping on the girl's back and slapping her hands over the girl's eyes.

The girl whirled around wildly, waving her knife.

Katie scrambled to her feet. "Come on!" she cried, pulling Lee off the girl. Together, they bolted for the back door.

"I'm gonna cut you!" screamed the girl. "Cut you both!"

Katie's legs pumped hard as she tore out into the schoolyard. "Hurry up," she shouted back at Lee who panted along behind her. "Come on!"

The girl with the knife burst through the back door.

Lee picked up her pace and caught up with Katie. "I can't run," she panted. "My side hurts too much."

"Hang onto me," said Katie.

Lee collapsed into her, and Katie caught her around the waist. Walking rapidly, they continued around to the front of the shelter. Katie kept checking behind her. The girl didn't seem to be coming after them.

"Let's just get out of here," Lee whispered.

Katie agreed. It wouldn't be smart to try to go back inside. They continued out to the entrance of the school and then turned right, continuing up Creek Road. "It was great the way you jumped on that girl," she said, forcing a laugh.

"I had to do something," Lee said weakly. Straightening suddenly, she stopped and pounded one fist into her other hand. "My stuff!" Lee cried. "My bag is back there."

Katie chuckled bitterly. "I missed my train and lost my pack, we almost got stabbed, we blew our chance of getting you to a nurse and eating—all because of that bag. And now it's gone."

"Well, we tried, anyway," said Lee, shaking her head wearily.

"Tried and failed," Katie added gloomily. "The good news is that I still have seventy-five cents in my back pocket."

"And a train ticket," Lee said.

"With more than two hours to kill until the train comes," Katie said with a shiver. The cold was now very bitter. "Where can we go to keep warm until then?"

At that moment snow began to fall.

"We'd better go somewhere—we can't stay out in this for the next two hours," said Lee, holding out her bare hand to catch a snowflake. "The train station?"

"What will you do after I get on the train?"

Lee shrugged. "I'll think of something."

Katie looked at her with a long, searching glance. What could she possibly think of? She was very sick. She had no money, no food, not even a pair of gloves. If she got stuck out in this snow, she'd probably get pneumonia. Or worse.

"Why don't we try to walk into town," Katie suggested. "For seventy-five cents, we could split a hot dog or something, at least."

"Okay," Lee agreed. "I think I can walk on my own now. Which way is town, do you think?"

"Well," Katie considered. "We know it's not back that way, toward the station. So it's got to be this way."

"Makes sense," said Lee. "Let's go."

"All right, but lean on me if you feel bad again," said Katie.

As they continued uphill, the snow fell ever more heavily. Katie clapped her raw, cold-reddened hands together for warmth. She sure hoped this road led into town. Even though they had another hour or more until it got dark, the sky was so heavy with snow it already looked like dusk. And it seemed to be getting colder by the moment.

"Where are you from?" Katie asked, peering straight ahead into the whirling snow.

She was answered with the sound of Lee's coughing, coming from behind her. Katie turned and saw Lee several yards away, leaning on a tree.

Katie went back to her and immediately saw that she looked worse than before. "Come on, you're going to freeze if you stay still," she urged Lee.

"You know, I'm not even cold," Lee said.

Katie felt Lee's forehead. "You sure aren't. You're burning up with a fever. This is crazy. We've got to get you to a hospital."

"But I have no money."

"We'll worry about that later. In the shape you're in, they've got to take you."

Lee slumped down to a sitting position at the base of the tree. "I don't think I can walk another step," she told Katie.

Katie stooped down beside her. "You found the energy to jump on that girl. Now you have to find the energy to keep going."

"I think that may have been my last blast of strength," Lee said weakly.

Katie had to admit that Lee did look wiped out. Her face was even paler than before. Her eyes had a peculiar, feverish brightness to them.

She took Lee's arm and gently drew her back up. Katie stepped forward, supporting Lee by the elbow. "You can do it," she urged her. "Come on, you *have* to."

Lee stumbled forward, then stopped and clutched her ribs.

Katie put her arm around Lee's waist. "Just lean on me. It can't be too far."

"I can't go any further. Really," Lee insisted weakly, sitting at the roadside.

"Then you'll have to wait here while I get help," said Katie. "I'll call a taxi and have the driver take us to the hospital."

"We don't have money," said Lee, closing her eyes.

"We won't tell him that until we're out of the cab."

Lee didn't answer. Her eyes remained closed. Katie knew she had to do something quickly. "Get up, Lee, please. You can't sit here in the snow."

Katie squatted down in front of Lee with her back to her. "Climb on," she said.

"You won't be able to carry me," Lee protested.

"Sure I will. I bet you're light as a feather," Katie assured her "Get on." Lee wrapped her arms around Katie's shoulders. Katie grabbed hold of them as she staggered to her feet. Lee *wasn't* light as a feather, but Katie hoped she could manage.

Carrying her that way, on piggyback, Katie continued up Creek Road. Within minutes, her back and shoulders began to ache under Lee's weight.

The snow now whirled around her. Katie had to keep her head down against the wind and stinging bits of ice mixed in with the snow.

When she turned a bend in the road she was able to make out the outline of a small building. A wooden sign suspended from a pole banged back and forth in the wind. Squinting against the snow, Katie could just make out the lettering. Nagle's Convenience Store, she read. "We're in luck," she told Lee. Lee didn't answer.

Katie picked up her pace, anxious to get to the store. But when she drew closer, she sighed with disappointment. A Closed sign sat in the window.

Holding Lee tightly, Katie leaned against the cold glass door. The road ahead was aswirl with snow. Katie had no idea what to do next.

Suddenly, Katie jumped away from the door. A man was coming around the side of the building.

21

The tall man passed them by on his way to a parked car, which was already coated with a layer of snow. He had a wide face beneath his cap and broad shoulders.

"Hey, mister!" Katie called out to him.

He turned toward her and waited.

"Do you know where I could find a taxi around here?" she shouted.

"You just found one," the man called back. With his gloved hand, he wiped snow away from the side of the car, revealing the words Nagle's Taxi. "Do you have money?" he asked.

"Sure," Katie answered. After all, she did have *some* money, although not nearly enough.

"Come on, then," the man said. "Get in."

Lee's eyes fluttered open as Katie dragged her toward the taxi. "What's happening?" she mumbled.

"We're getting a ride to a hospital," Katie told her. She pulled open the back door and shifted her weight so that Lee tumbled onto the seat. Instantly, Lee stretched out on the back seat, tucking her hands under her cheek. Katie had no room to get in, so she went around to the passenger side of the taxi and slid in next to the driver.

"Where to?" he asked pleasantly.

"The nearest hospital, please," said Katie. "My friend is pretty sick."

The man checked over his shoulder and nodded. "She doesn't look too good," he concurred, starting the engine. "Miller's Creek doesn't have its own hospital. We could take you over to County General, or . . . well, don't worry, we'll get you to a hospital."

"Please," said Katie, rubbing her hands together. "I think she might have pneumonia."

The taxi driver turned on the heat. The blast from the vent made Katie's fingers tingle for a moment as she gratefully held her numbed hand up to it. "Boy, you don't appreciate warmth until you go without it," she said.

The man nodded. "A lot of things in life are like that."

"I guess so," Katie replied. Now that she was beside him, she took a closer look at the driver. He was younger than she'd thought at first, in his twenties, with a friendly face and a wide, slightly crooked nose that looked as if it might have been broken at one time.

The wipers went on with a steady, dull, *thunk-thunk.* The driver headed up Creek Road. "Where are your parents?" the driver asked.

"Mine are dead," Katie replied quietly.

"So are mine," said the man. "But, you know, I often get a feeling that they're nearby."

Katie sat forward. "You do?"

"Uh–huh."

"I bet you feel dumb afterwards, though, don't you?"

The driver shook his head as he navigated around a garbage can that had blown out into the road. "No. I believe they're really there."

"Really?"

"Yeah. I don't think love dies."

"How do you feel . . . what's it like when you think they're around you?" Katie needed to know.

The driver frowned thoughtfully. "It's a good feeling. I suddenly get the idea that I've found a spot of calm and tranquility. When I step into that spot, the calmness comes over me, too. I feel their love, and it gives me new energy to face my problems."

"Do they speak to you or appear or anything like that?"

The driver shook his head. "It's just a feeling."

"I had a feeling like that not long ago," Katie admitted.

"Did it make you happy?" the driver asked.

"No, it made me confused. In fact, I felt like a jerk, like I'd been . . . I don't know, *had* or something."

"That's because you didn't trust the feeling. Next time it happens, just let their love wash over you. You'll see what I mean."

"How do I know there *will* be a next time?" Katie asked.

"There will be," the driver said confidently. "They won't give up on you, even if you've given up on them."

Katie nodded. "If I could believe that, I wouldn't feel so alone."

"Believe it," said the driver.

Katie peered out the window. The headlights now lit only about one car-length in front of them, shining on a curtain of falling whiteness. "Can you see where we're going?" Katie asked.

"I'm taking it slow," the driver assured her.

Katie checked on Lee in the backseat. She mumbled and shifted in her sleep. "I hope she's all right," Katie said anxiously.

They continued driving through the blinding snow for what seemed like another half hour. "No offense, but do you know where you're going?" Katie asked, getting worried.

The driver nodded. "I know."

Katie squinted at him suspiciously. "Are you sure you know your way around here? How long have you been driving this taxi?"

"Long enough," he laughed.

Katie folded her arms and sat back in the seat. It seemed like they'd been driving for hours. He was very nice, but what did she really know about him? Maybe he was some kind of nut. Maybe this wasn't even really his cab. What if he'd just robbed the people in the Nagle Convenience Store and had taken the keys to the taxi?

Looking out the window, Katie could barely see anything. She began to wish they'd come to a main road with stores and lights. The driver seemed to be keeping entirely on the back roads.

"Shouldn't we have come to a hospital by now?" Katie questioned after another while had passed.

"Do you think so?" the driver asked.

"Yeah, I *do* think so," said Katie, getting scared. He

was supposed to be a taxi driver. Didn't he know his way around.

Maybe she should have thought twice before getting into a cab that just happened to be sitting there like that. What if this guy tricked people into getting into the car with him by pretending to be a cab driver?

She glanced at the cab's dashboard. There was no identifying cab license, no radio, none of the stuff you usually saw in regular taxi cabs.

Who was this guy, really? And where, exactly, was he taking them?

22

As if in answer to her question, a bright white sign appeared, shining through the curtain of snow.

"Pine Ridge Hospital?" Katie exclaimed. "*This* is the closest hospital you could find?"

"I guess it was," said the driver, pulling into the garishly-lit emergency entrance. "You wanted a hospital, and I got you to one. You owe me seventy-five cents."

"That's all?" Katie couldn't believe it.

"Special blizzard rates?" The driver laughed.

Katie looked at him long and hard. "How did you know that's how much I have?"

"Good guess."

Just then, a young woman with blonde hair, wearing a coat and with a stethoscope around her neck, rapped on the taxi window by Katie. When Katie rolled the window down, she leaned in to talk. "I'm Dr. Dewain. Do you need assistance here? I see this girl passed out in the back."

"Thanks! Yes, we do," Katie said. "I think she has

pneumonia or something."

Lee sat up groggily in the backseat. "Where are we?" she rasped.

"At the hospital. You're going to be all right," Katie told her.

Dr. Dewain opened the back door and helped Lee out. "This girl is burning with fever," she said, alarmed. "Someone will have to look after her right away." The woman drew Lee out of the taxi and put her arm around her.

Katie hopped out to help. She was almost to the hospital entrance with Lee and Dr. Dewain when she remembered she hadn't paid the driver.

He stood in the snow by the curb outside his taxi.

"I owe you seventy-five cents!" she cried, heading back.

"Go ahead with your friend," he shouted. "I'm going to get coffee. I'll be here awhile."

"Okay. I'll be right back," Katie said gratefully. He was really nice. She felt guilty for having doubted him.

Katie pushed in the heavy glass hospital door and discovered that Dr. Dewain and Lee hadn't waited for her. She searched the lobby, turning in a circle. How had they gotten so far so fast?

Katie went to a desk marked Admitting. A nurse sitting behind the desk smiled kindly at her. "Could you please tell me where Dr. Dewain took my friend?"

"Doctor who?" asked the nurse.

"Dewain."

The nurse looked at some papers on her desk. "I'm not familiar with that doctor, and I don't see the name here. What's your friend's name?"

"Lee—uh—. Wow. I don't know," Katie was embarrassed to admit.

"A Mr. Fong Lee was admitted an hour ago," the nurse said, checking her list.

"No, that's not her," Katie told her.

"There's no other Lee here on my list. I'm sorry."

"Thanks anyway," said Katie. She wandered away from the desk and looked down a long white corridor. She just had to find Lee or Dr. Dewain.

"Katie!"

Katie recognized the voice calling her name and whirled around.

"Ashley!" she cried in surprise.

Ashley ran to her and hugged her hard. Icy snow flecked her coppery curls. "Are you all right?"

"Yeah. What are you doing here?"

"Looking for you."

"How did you know I was here?"

"Your aunt and uncle came to the ranch looking for you. They showed up about an hour ago, and just as they pulled up in front of my house my mother got this phone call from a man saying that you were here at the hospital."

"Who could have called?" Katie asked in disbelief. "Only the taxi driver knew we were here, and we've been in the car with him for at least an hour."

"Well, *someone* called," Ashley insisted. "We asked your aunt and uncle if we could come, too, and then we came over here as fast as possible."

"*We?*" Katie asked.

"Christina went in the opposite direction from me.

When they told us you hadn't been admitted, we all spread out to look for you."

"Why were you so sure I was here?"

"Well, your aunt and uncle and I weren't. But Christina said she felt a strong vibration telling her you were here."

At that moment, Christina appeared at the far end of the hall. "I knew it! I knew it!" she cried, hurrying toward them, her purple cape flying behind her. When she reached Katie, she hugged her with her good left arm. "You look all right. Are you?"

"Hi. Yeah. I'm okay. Listen, are my aunt and uncle ready to murder me?" Katie needed to know.

"No. They're really upset, though. Your aunt keeps crying and telling your uncle it's all his fault that you ran away," Ashley reported. "He keeps mumbling and saying everything will be all right once they find you, but they have to find you first."

Katie was surprised by how glad she was to hear this news. After what she'd been through today and what she'd seen of Lee's life, and life at the shelter, her time with Aunt Rainie and Uncle Jeff didn't seem as horrible as it had. It wasn't great—but now she knew it could be a lot worse. "Where are they?" she asked.

"We left them in the lobby," said Christina.

"I guess we'd better tell them I'm here," said Katie.

They walked quickly back to the lobby, but Aunt Rainie and Uncle Jeff weren't there. "They've probably gone off to look for you somewhere else," Ashley guessed.

"You two wait here while I go pay the taxi driver,"

said Katie. "I want to ask him who called your house, anyway. He's the only one who could know."

Ashley grabbed Katie's sleeve. "You really will come back, won't you?"

Katie smiled. "I'm not going anywhere in this blizzard. Besides, I want to come back and find a girl I came in here with. I've sort of lost track of her." She headed out the hospital door and saw the taxi, still by the curb and rapidly piling up with snow. But the driver wasn't in it, and she didn't see him nearby.

Turning up her collar, Katie headed out of the doorway and into the snow, keeping to the cement path surrounding the building. She turned the corner of the hospital building and came to what appeared to be a service entrance for the hospital cafeteria.

There she stopped short, totally confused by the sight before her.

Lee, Dr. Dewain, and the cab driver all stood in the snow, smiling and talking. Lee didn't seem a bit sick anymore. And Dr. Dewain wasn't wearing a coat, only a doctor's jacket. The cab driver turned toward Katie and smiled warmly.

"Katie, there you are!" cried Ashley. She and Christina were running toward Katie through the falling snow. "Your aunt and uncle are in the lobby and they told us to get you and . . ." Ashley's voiced trailed off as she got nearer.

Katie turned. "What are you looking at?" she asked. "You're expression is so—"

"Oh, my! Oh, my!" Christina murmured, her blue eyes wide.

Ashley and Christina were staring past Katie, transfixed.

Katie turned back to see what they were looking at, and her breath caught in her throat.

Lee, Dr. Dewain, and the taxi driver had been transformed into Norma, Edwina, and Ned—only now they glowed with an unearthly light.

And they had wings!

Giant, shimmering wings. The majestic white light enveloped them from the tips of their flowing hair to the hems of their silvery white gowns.

They were beautiful. The most gorgeous, amazing sight Katie had ever seen, could ever imagine seeing.

Their smiles radiated joy. Then, with a soft *swoosh* of their robes, they began to float upward. They looked at the girls, their identical violet blue eyes suffused with love.

And then they were gone.

23

Dear Journal,

I'm back with Aunt Rainie and Uncle Jeff again. We had a long (long!) talk and sorted a lot of stuff out. I think we all understand one another a lot better now. Life here still isn't my idea of great. It sure isn't as good as the life I had back on West 68th Street. But I've decided to stop looking for what isn't here and pay attention to what is. After all, they *did* come out in a blizzard and look for me. That must count for something.

They're even letting me keep one of Myrtle's kittens. And get this—it was Uncle Jeff's idea. Can you believe it? He says, "Caring for an animal teaches responsibility." I'm beginning to think that he's not really as mean as he seems, but that maybe he's mean enough not to want anyone to think he's not mean. If you know what I mean. Ha-ha.

I know this sounds weird, but the kitten I'm keeping has sort of blue-green eyes that remind me a little bit of the Galens—you know, the angels. I've named it Nagle.

Some things about living in a small town aren't all bad. The train conductor found my backpack and returned it to the train station. The ticket seller found out who I was—that's one of the not-so-great things about life in a small town: you have no privacy. Anyway, he returned it, and all my stuff was still there. I'm keeping the picture of my parents out where I can see it. It kind of makes me feel like they're watching over me.

Well, my trip didn't turn out at all like I planned. But the few hours I was away was an unbelievable adventure. I could probably write ten stories about the things that happened. Although I didn't travel a zillion miles, it felt like I was on a long, long journey.

I might not turn into that nasty person I was worried about becoming, after all.

She shut her journal and took out a box of stationery. Maybe she'd write one last letter to Addy.

No. There was no sense in it. Addy obviously didn't want a friend who lived so far away. Besides, her life was here now. Addy belonged to a different time and place. If they'd been true friends, it might not have mattered. But Addy hadn't turned out to be the friend Katie had thought she was.

So much hadn't turned out the way Katie expected.

Katie sat on the end of her bed and pictured the gorgeous angels in her mind's eye. She hadn't been able to think of much else.

The door downstairs slammed. Moments later, Katie heard footsteps approaching her room. "Hi," said Ashley, poking her head in the door. Christina was right behind her.

Katie noticed that they were both barefoot. "Where are your shoes?" she asked.

"We left them downstairs because they were so muddy," Ashley explained. "It's so warm out, everything is melting like crazy. It's a mess."

"Do you want to know how I feel?" asked Christina as she unbuttoned her cape. "I feel like the first astronaut on the moon must have felt. After you've walked on the moon—after you've experienced something that mind-meltingly awesome—how can you ever be the same again?"

"You can't be," Katie answered promptly, sure she was right.

"I think so, too," Ashley agreed, sitting on Katie's bed. "You can't be."

"We asked the angels to help you, you know," Christina told Katie.

"Well, they did!" said Katie. "Thanks."

Christina sat on the bed beside Ashley. "It's so amazing that I'm having a hard time even thinking about it," she said.

"I know what you mean," said Ashley.

"But I can't think about anything else," added Katie.

"The three of us are feeling the same way," said Christina. "I wonder if we'll ever see them again. And I wonder if they've been with us all along."

Katie thought about the angel who'd stopped her from being hit by a car when she was five. Now she knew that face. It had been Norma's face.

But Norma was young now. How could she have been young then, too?

Maybe angels didn't deal with time the same way we do, Katie considered. Maybe they dropped in and out of years the same way we step in and out of puddles.

Perhaps angels were just always there—forever.

"I wonder about those things, too," Katie answered Christina. "But at least all three of us saw them. We know we're not crazy, and we can talk to each other about it if we need to. Right?"

"Right," Ashley agreed.

"Right," said Christina with a smile.

Katie beamed at her friends. It had been a hard winter, but now she was sure spring was coming at last.

FOREVER ANGELS

by Suzanne Weyn

Everyone needs a special angel . . .

Available wherever you buy books.

Troll

FOREVER ANGELS

ASHLEY'S LOST ANGEL

by Suzanne Weyn

Ashley's searching for a miracle

Perfect Ashley's perfect life is suddenly falling apart. The boy she likes doesn't like her anymore, her grades are sinking, and her horse is sick. But that's nothing compared to her parents' problems. Their money troubles may force them to close their horse farm and give up the only home Ashley's ever known. Worst of all, they're even talking about getting a divorce. Ashley's desperate for an answer, something that can turn her life around. Is anyone listening?

Available wherever you buy books.

Troll

FOREVER ANGELS

CHRISTINA'S DANCING ANGEL

by Suzanne Weyn

All she wants to do is dance . . . like an angel

Christina dreams of dancing on air, but reality
keeps bringing her down to earth. Her dance
teacher thinks Christina should give it up, that
Christina will never have the right build for
dancing. Christina thinks where there's a will
there's a way. If she can only make herself over,
she's sure her wishes will come true. Her friends
liked the old Christina just fine, and they're
worried she's trying too hard to change. Christina
is truly more special than anyone can guess, least
of all Christina, but it will take a special being to
make her see the light.

Available wherever you buy books.

Troll

FOREVER ANGELS

THE BABY ANGEL

by Suzanne Weyn

**Who is this darling baby—
and where did she come from?**

Aunt Rainie and Uncle Jeff have gone away on
vacation, and Katie can't help remembering her
real parents. They went away, too, but they never
came back. Now Katie feels abandoned all over
again. Then, on a walk in the woods, Katie finds
a tiny baby crying in a clearing. Katie can't find
the parents, and she can't leave the baby. Finally,
she decides the only thing she can do is bring
the baby home with her. But this is no ordinary
baby . . .

Available wherever you buy books.

Troll

FOREVER ANGELS

AN ANGEL FOR MOLLY

by Suzanne Weyn

**This little rich girl has everything—
except what she really wants the most**

Molly is thrilled. Her father has decided to let her join him on a business trip, and they'll be staying in an ancient Irish castle. She's hoping she can use the extra time with her father to talk about some things that are really important to her. Once they arrive in Ireland, though, Molly's father is distant and preoccupied. So Molly comes up with a reckless plan to get his attention. But when the plan backfires horribly, who can save Molly—and help her find her heart's desire?

Available wherever you buy books.

Troll